"You are, hands down, one of the most impressive women I've ever known."

"I bet you say that to all the girls who could break your nose with one punch."

"Nope. Just you."

Then Pete leaned forward and, despite all of Chloe's resolve not to kiss him, her eyes fluttered closed in anticipation and one word floated through her mind—*finally*.

But instead of feeling his lips against hers, he kissed her on the forehead.

Which was good. Great, even. She pushed down the disappointment.

Pete turned and headed back to the bar. "Stay here and try not to get into any more fights."

"They started it!" she called after him.

"But you finished it like a *boss*." There was no mistaking the approval in his voice.

Oh, heavens.

Was she starting to like Pete Wellington?

What else could go w

His Enemy's
First Fam
from Sa

Dear Reader,

Welcome to the All-Stars rodeo, an all-around circuit owned by the Lawrence family. Three siblings run the rodeo—but not everyone loves it.

Since she was a teenager, Chloe Lawrence has been the princess of the rodeo, riding out before every rodeo with the flag. But she's more than just a pretty face—she wants to take on a management role with the All-Stars. And her family is finally giving her the chance to prove herself.

There's only one problem—and he's six-two with a huge chip on his shoulder. Pete Wellington's father lost the All-Stars to Chloe's father in a poker game and Pete wants it back. He's tried everything and nothing's worked. His only option? Get a job working for his enemy—which means working for Chloe Lawrence.

Except she's not some pretty city slicker—Chloe really cares about the All-Stars. When a fight threatens to sink the All-Stars, Pete and Chloe have no choice but to work together. And the more time he spends with her, the more he sees not his enemy's daughter but a woman he can't stay away from. But when Chloe's father finds out about Pete's rodeo job, all hell breaks loose. Pete may finally get what he wants—the rodeo—but will he have to give up Chloe to get it?

His Enemy's Daughter is a sensual story about fighting for your dreams and falling in love. I hope you enjoy reading this book as much as I enjoyed writing it! Be sure to stop by sarahmanderson.com and sign up for my newsletter at eepurl.com/nv39b to join me as I say, "Long live cowboys!"

Sarah

SARAH M. ANDERSON

HIS ENEMY'S DAUGHTER

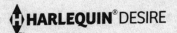

Recycling programs
for this product may
not exist in your area.

ISBN-13: 978-1-335-97162-3

His Enemy's Daughter

Copyright © 2018 by Sarah M. Anderson

This edition published by arrangement with Harlequin Books S.A.

For questions and comments about the quality of this book, please contact us at CustomerService@Harlequin.com.

® and TM are trademarks of Harlequin Enterprises Limited or its corporate affiliates. Trademarks indicated with ® are registered in the United States Patent and Trademark Office, the Canadian Intellectual Property Office and in other countries.

Printed in U.S.A.

Sarah M. Anderson may live east of the Mississippi River, but her heart lies out west on the Great Plains. Sarah's book *A Man of Privilege* won an *RT Book Reviews* Reviewers' Choice Best Book Award in 2012. *The Nanny Plan* was a 2016 RITA® Award winner for Contemporary Romance: Short.

Sarah spends her days having conversations with imaginary cowboys and billionaires. Find out more about Sarah's heroes at sarahmanderson.com and sign up for the new-release newsletter at eepurl.com/nv39b.

Books by Sarah M. Anderson

Harlequin Desire

The Beaumont Heirs

Not the Boss's Baby
Tempted by a Cowboy
A Beaumont Christmas
His Son, Her Secret
Falling for Her Fake Fiancé
His Illegitimate Heir
Rich Rancher for Christmas

First Family of Rodeo

His Best Friend's Sister
His Enemy's Daughter

Visit her Author Profile page at Harlequin.com, or sarahmanderson.com, for more titles.

To Kristi—I'm so glad you've come into our lives!

One

It took everything Chloe Lawrence had to keep her winning smile locked into place.

"Miss," the stock contractor said, taking off his hat and slicking his thin hair back before replacing the Stetson, "this isn't how we did things back when your father was in charge."

The first time some grizzled old coot had said that to her, she had been genuinely shocked. For all intents and purposes, Milt Lawrence hadn't been in charge of the All-Around All-Stars Pro Rodeo since her brother Oliver had wrestled control of the family empire away from the older man four years ago. The All-Stars was one of the family's many holdings, had been ever since her father had won the rodeo circuit in a poker game thirteen years ago.

Oliver had managed the rodeo from a distance while simultaneously running their main company, Lawrence Energies. Which meant that, on the ground, Chloe was the Lawrence the stock contractors had been dealing with.

"Mort," she said, keeping her voice warm and friendly instead of angry. "This is just a slight change in who's qualified to compete."

Which was not necessarily the truth.

Allowing women to compete with the men was anything but *slight*. But it wasn't like she was suggesting they cut calf-roping or anything.

Dale Jenkins, an older man with his stomach hanging over his belt buckle, stepped in front of Mort. "What Mort is trying to say," he drawled, "is that of *course* we're still interested in supplying the All-Stars with our stock. But you're *just* the Princess of the Rodeo. You're good at it, of course," he added, as if that somehow made it better. "But…"

He aimed a big smile at her, one that Chloe recognized. But that *just* grated on her every nerve.

When she'd been younger and so excited to open and close every rodeo, Dale had given her that exact same smile and patted her on the head as if she were a puppy and told her that she looked "right pretty up on that horse."

If he patted her on the head now, she might break his hand.

"Gentlemen," she said, putting as much force as she could into the word. "There is no harm in trying something different. If it works, the All-Stars will gain viewers, fans and sales. When those three things combine, you know what that gets us?" She waved her hand to encompass Dale, Mort and the other cowboys paying attention. "More money. A rising tide lifts all boats."

"Women ride barrels," said a crusty old fart named Dustin Yardley. He stalked right into her personal space. "You're asking us to be part and parcel of something we didn't sign up for. The All-Stars is a men's rodeo." He gave her a look that was so mean she had to fight the urge to take a step back. She wouldn't show fear before these men.

Of course, meanness was Dustin's natural look, so it was hard for Chloe to tell if he was extra condescending today or not. "And we," he went on, "are the *men* who make the rodeo work."

Oh, that absolutely did it. She had heard some version of that speech in Des Moines, Kansas City, Shreveport, Memphis and, worst of all, in Fort Worth. Now she was hearing it in Sikeston, Missouri.

None of the stock contractors or riders or promoters had ever had an issue with her running the All-Stars when her brother Oliver or her father, Milt, were nominally in charge. All she'd had to do then was phrase her orders as coming from her family.

From a man.

But this year was different. At the beginning of the season, Oliver had ceded all control, real or imagined, to Chloe. He was way too busy to handle the All-Stars. He'd gone and fallen in love with Chloe's oldest friend, Renee Preston—who came with a certain amount of scandal, what with her being pregnant with her dead husband's child and the rest of her family under indictment for running a massive pyramid scheme.

And besides, Oliver *hated* the rodeo. Chloe still didn't understand why. She loved it and she'd been pushing for more control over the All-Stars for years. It hadn't been until Oliver had gone behind their father's back to give her the television distribution negotiations that she'd been able to prove her skills.

And prove them, she had. She wasn't *just* the Princess of the Rodeo. Not anymore.

Or so she'd thought.

This season should have been Chloe's victory tour. Finally, the rodeo she'd loved since her father had won it was hers and hers alone. The TV deal was just the first step. She'd also launched her own line of couture cowgirl clothing named—what else?— Princess of the Rodeo and it was selling well. Sure, the workload was insane and yeah, she didn't get much sleep anymore. But her brother had managed the rodeo while running a billion-dollar energy corporation. She could juggle some cowboys and clothing. She *had* to—this was just the beginning.

She had plans. Great plans.

Plans that required people to go along with them.

The one variable she hadn't accounted for. Damned people.

She gritted her teeth. "*Mister* Yardley," she said. She didn't have time to stand around debating. She just needed them to nod and smile and say they'd be happy to try something new. "I'll be sure to pass that sentiment along to your wife and two daughters, who delivered the agreed-upon calves to the Bootheel Rodeo last year—by themselves—while you were recovering from surgery. How's the heart, by the way?" She did her best to look sweet and concerned.

Not that Yardley was buying it. His eyes narrowed as his lip curled. He was not a man who took kindly to having his authority questioned, especially not by someone who was just a *princess*. "Now you look here, missy," he began, his cheeks darkening.

That's when a male voice behind her said, "Problem?"

Inside, her heart sank.

If she had expected anyone to barge into this situation, it would have been her younger brother, Flash Lawrence. He was not only a Lawrence heir but also a cowboy who rode for the All-Stars. He was legendary for three things—his charm with the ladies, the chip on his shoulder and his short-fuse temper.

She'd had plenty of trouble in Omaha when, in the middle of a similar conversation with similar contractors, Flash had decided Chloe's honor needed to be defended. It had taken all of her negotiating skills to get the police to drop the charges.

She would be so lucky if it was Flash who'd spoken. But today was not her lucky day.

Yardley smirked as he made eye contact with the man standing behind Chloe. The very last man she wanted to deal with. She would take a hundred Jenkinses and Yardleys and Gandys rather than deal with this *one* man.

"Pete Wellington," Yardley said and Chloe didn't miss the sudden warmth and good cheer in his voice. "What a surprise to see you here."

He didn't sound surprised. In fact, none of the men she'd been trying to reason with looked shocked that Pete Wellington had ventured from his East Texas ranch to drop by the All-Stars rodeo in Missouri.

Dammit.

"How've you been?" Mort asked, then he cut a glance at Chloe. "We'd love to see you at the rodeo again."

Yeah, that wasn't subtle. But before she could point out that Pete Wellington hadn't had jack crap to do with the All-Stars in years, Dale spoke. "You here to compete?" he asked, beaming widely. "We sure do miss seeing a *real* professional in the arena."

Lord, why didn't they just roll out a red carpet and lick his boots clean? Chloe had to fight back a scream of frustration. She didn't like it when people took pot shots at Flash, but the fact was he was a damned good rider. He'd earned that seventh-place world ranking on his own, no matter what anyone else thought.

"Now, gentlemen," Pete said from behind her and she had to repress a shiver at the sound of his voice, deep and rich. "You know I retired from riding years ago."

"Doesn't mean you can't make a comeback. It'd be an improvement. A *huge* one." Yardley started to step around her to shake Wellington's hand, but Chloe wasn't having any of it. Pete's father, Davey Wellington, might have founded this rodeo, but he'd also lost it fair and square in a poker game to Chloe's father, Milt.

She wasn't going to let anyone cut her out of *her* rodeo. Especially not Pete Wellington.

Just as Yardley stuck out his hand, Chloe spun to face her nemesis, *accidentally* hip-checking Yardley. "Whoops," she said, working hard to keep her eyes innocent when Dustin stumbled. "Why, Mr. Wellington," she cooed. She'd once heard Flash call him that and Pete had snapped that *Mister* Wellington was his father and she absolutely wasn't above using every single weapon at her disposal. She batted her eyelashes and shifted so her breasts were at their best before finishing, "I didn't see you join us!"

She looked up at him through her lashes—a move that usually gave her total control over the situation. But Pete Wellington wasn't distracted by a pretty face. If that were possible, she would have had him eating out of her hands for the last ten years.

Instead, he said, "Well, well, well. If it isn't the Princess of the Rodeo." His tone was only slightly mocking. "You've got things well in hand, I see. As usual."

Chloe refused to react. She didn't even allow her cheeks to heat as the old farts around her started chuckling. She'd been performing in public as the Princess of the Rodeo since she was sixteen, three years after her dad had taken over the circuit. Every weekend, at the featured All-Around All-Stars Rodeo, Chloe opened and closed the show by riding a horse into the arena and carrying a huge American flag.

The All-Stars was the big leagues for cowboys who wanted to demonstrate their skills at calf-roping, bronco-busting, team roping, steer wrestling *and* bull riding. It didn't bring in as much money as the Total Bull Challenge, which was strictly bull riding. But Chloe had plans to change that.

The first step was to find her breakout star— who was absolutely not her brother Flash. She'd love to find a female rider, a positive role model to bring in younger girls. After all, that strategy had worked wonders for the Total Bull Challenge's bottom line when June Spotted Elk had worked her way up through the ranks. Why shouldn't Chloe replicate that success?

Pete smirked down at her while Dustin chortled behind her. They were the reason that, at this very moment, she wasn't replicating any success.

She *hated* Pete Wellington and his smug attitude and his built body, not to mention his freaking amazing jaw that only looked better with a five-o'clock shadow. And his eyes! They were almost gray when he looked down at her from under the brim of his brown cowboy hat but, depending on the light, changed to either light blue or green. Oh, how she hated Pete's eyes in particular. They were simply the most beautiful color she'd ever seen and some days, all she wanted to do was stare into them endlessly and watch them shift with the changing light.

But more than that, she hated the way he looked at her. Would it kill him to acknowledge that she was a damned good steward to his beloved rodeo? That she ran a tight ship and got things done—like television distribution and increased revenues?

Apparently, it would kill him because she only saw mocking contempt in his eyes. His lips curved into something that could have been a heart-stopping smile on a man with a soul but on him was nothing but a taunting sneer.

He was in Missouri for one reason and one reason alone—to knock her down in front of the very men she most needed to buy into her new plans.

If that's how he wanted to play this, fine. It wasn't her fault his father hadn't been able to hold his liquor. Nor was it her fault that the man had been a lousy poker player who hadn't known when to hold 'em or when to fold 'em. But Pete acted as if she'd stolen his rodeo. As if she'd been there, pouring Davey Wellington another shot of whiskey and whispering in his ear.

Basically, he looked at her like she was the devil incarnate and he treated her accordingly.

She was only too happy to return the favor.

"It's true I have much more to get my hands around than you do," she replied easily, keeping everything light, as if she weren't intentionally insulting his manhood. "But it's so nice to see you getting out and about again." She patted his upper arm, pointedly not noticing the way his hard biceps tensed at her casual touch. "You let me know if you need any help dealing with the crowds. I know it can be overwhelming if you're not used to it."

Any hint of a smirk on his nice, full lips died, which only made her smile broaden. But instead of launching a counterattack, Pete swallowed hard and said, "Big night?"

"Been sold out for weeks." Of course, part of that was because Dwight Yoakam was the closing act. It'd been a huge get, bringing a country star of that magnitude to this tiny corner of Missouri.

But she was going to put on a hell of a rodeo while she had butts in the seats. She had to. If this didn't work…no. There was no *if* here. It would absolutely work. When the rodeo took off, she'd be the one holding the reins.

She braced herself. Now he would come up firing. Now he would try to destroy her with a witty comeback. She could see the cords on his neck straining as he ground his teeth. No matter what he said, she wouldn't let him get to her.

Now. Surely *now*.

"Pete, maybe you can make the little lady see sense," Mort said.

"About what?" Pete replied, but he didn't look away from her.

"About women," Dustin said. He whipped his hat off his head and slapped it against his leg. "She doesn't know what she's talking about."

Pete stepped back and looked Chloe up and down, his gaze traveling the path over her blinged-out cowgirl shirt and customized jeans—both from her Princess of the Rodeo clothing line—way too slowly for her taste. "I don't know, guys. She looks pretty qualified in the woman department, if you ask me."

Chloe blushed. She didn't want to, didn't want Pete to know that his words could affect her at all—but she couldn't help it. Was he…protecting her? Or just ogling her?

What was going on?

"She wants to let women compete!" Dustin all but roared.

"Don't get us wrong," Dale went on in his pleasantly condescending voice, "women can ride the hell out of barrels."

"And they're good-looking," Mort unhelpfully added.

Chloe managed not to lose her ever-loving mind. But she couldn't stop herself from gritting her teeth and closing her eyes. Their words shouldn't hurt. They wouldn't.

"But you put a pretty little thing out there in the arena with a man and he's gonna get distracted," Dustin said, disgust in his voice. "And a distracted cowboy is a hurt cowboy. You know that, Pete."

Pete cleared his throat, making Chloe open her eyes again. He had to be *loving* this open rebellion. Hell, she wouldn't be surprised if he'd orchestrated this whole scene. She glanced around—yep. They'd amassed a crowd of about twenty people. Lovely. There would be plenty of witnesses to her humiliation.

At least Flash wasn't here. There wasn't a single bad situation her brother couldn't make worse.

Then the weirdest thing happened. Pete Wellington—a man who had never bothered to hide his hatred of her—lowered his chin and, from under the brim of his hat where no one else could see it, winked at her. Before she could figure what the hell *that* was supposed to mean, he stepped back.

"You're right," he said to Dustin in particular and the crowd of cowboys in general. "I happen to know firsthand that, because we don't have mixed competitions, no one has ever been injured in the All-Stars rodeo."

Chloe blinked. Was that…sarcasm?

In her *defense*?

What the hell was going on?

There was a three-second pause while Pete's words settled over the crowd before the first chuckle started. Another joined it and soon, all the guys who'd ridden in rodeos, past or present, began to laugh.

"Face it, boys," Pete went on, "we've all been stepped on by a bull or thrown by a bronco." Heads nodded in agreement. It was practically a sea of bobbing cowboy hats. "Women have nothing to do with the bones I've broken or the bruises I've suffered— no offense to my momma, who tried to keep me out of the arena. I say, if women want to compete on our teams and they can help a team win, why wouldn't we want that to happen?"

The bobbing stopped and Dustin pounced. "Are you serious, Wellington?"

"Have you ever seen my sister rope a steer?" Pete shot back. "She could give any man in this arena a run for his money."

Chloe stared almost helplessly up at Pete. He hadn't gone in for the kill. He really was defending her.

When he looked down at her, an electric shock skated over her skin. Then he completely blew her mind by saying, "If Chloe says it's a good idea to open up the team competitions to women, then it's a good idea."

"You can't seriously think *she's* had a good idea." Dustin spat into the dirt.

"Do I look like I'm joking?" Pete shot back.

Chloe gaped at the man.

Who the hell was this Pete damned Wellington?

Two

Pete couldn't remember the last time he'd had this much fun. Chloe Lawrence looked exactly like a fish stunned to find itself in the bottom of a boat instead of the bottom of a lake. By God, it was good to get the upper hand on the woman, for once. Everything was going according to plan.

Pete cut a glance back at Chloe. If he weren't enjoying himself quite so much, he'd be tempted to feel sorry for her. She was normally so high and mighty, the kind of smugly self-assured woman who thought she was better than everyone else, especially him. She never missed the opportunity to rub his face in the fact that the All-Stars wasn't his rodeo anymore.

Now he'd turned the tables and he was going to

enjoy rubbing her face in it. These men didn't owe her any particular allegiance and they all knew it.

But that fleeting moment when Dustin took a swipe at her, where pain etched her delicate features, didn't make him feel like he was winning. It made him feel like an ass. He felt like he'd seen that look before, a long time ago. Probably when he'd said something cruel. He couldn't remember what and besides, Chloe always gave as good as she got, so he wouldn't bother to feel bad about past insults.

He pushed back against that wisp of guilt because it was small and easily ignored. Hey, he was not the bad guy here, never had been. All he wanted was what was rightfully his. It had nothing to do with Chloe personally. It had everything to do with her lying, cheating family.

But even as he repeated that familiar truth, his gaze was drawn to her again. The fact that she was the most gorgeous woman he'd ever had the displeasure of butting heads with only made it worse. In another lifetime, the one where his family still owned the All-Stars, he and Chloe wouldn't be on opposite sides of a never-ending war. She would've been just another gorgeous face and Pete would've been free to...

Well, he would've had his rodeo back.

The rodeo was *his*, dammit. The Lawrence Oil All-Around All-Stars Pro Rodeo circuit was comprised of individual rodeos that were hosted from small towns to big cities. Most of the rodeos, like the Bootheel Rodeo in Missouri, predated the All-Stars by decades.

When Pete's father Davey had started the All-Stars back in the eighties with a group of his friends, he'd had big plans. More than just a bunch of individual rodeos—with individual winners—Davey Wellington had seen a way to crown the world's best All-Around Cowboy. It'd been a crazy idea but then, Davey had been just crazy enough to make it work.

Every rodeo that wanted to count toward the world rankings had to be approved by the All-Around All-Stars. The summers of Pete's childhood had been spent with his dad, driving from rodeo to rodeo to see if that local rodeo was worthy of being counted as an All-Star rodeo.

God, those had been good days, just the two of them in Dad's truck, sending postcards back to Mom. As far as he could recall, those summers had been the only time Pete had ever had his father's undivided attention. Pete might not have been there when Davey decided to settle the matter of who the best cowboy was forever, but by his father's side, Pete had literally worked to build the All-Stars from the ground up.

Rodeo was family. The All-Stars was *his* family, his father's legacy. It was his legacy, by God. Except for that damned poker game. Milt Lawrence had all but stolen the All-Stars from Davey when the man was deep into his whiskey and nothing Pete did could change that. And God knew he'd tried.

When Armstrong Oil—Lawrence Oil's main

competitor—had tapped oil on his ranch and Pete had suddenly become quite rich, he'd tried to buy the All-Stars back from Milt Lawrence. Hadn't worked. Neither had any of the lawsuits that had followed.

The Lawrences were like leeches. Once they'd latched on, they weren't letting go until they'd drained the All-Stars of all its history, meaning and money. It was time to try a new line of attack.

One that relied on grumpy old farts. "You can't be serious," Yardley snarled. "We had a deal."

Pete glared at the man. He should've known better than to trust Dustin Yardley with something like this.

"What deal?" Chloe snapped. Any trace of confusion was gone from her face. She jammed her hands on the sweet curve of her hips and glared at Pete. Because of course she suspected the truth.

It was no accident that Pete was in Missouri today and it was no accident that he'd come upon the scene with Chloe being browbeaten by a bunch of old cowboys.

"What deal?" Pete echoed, trying to sound innocent and hoping that Dustin would get the damned hint to shut his trap.

Chloe had been running the rodeo by herself for a few months now and the buck stopped with her. She couldn't hide behind her daddy's boots anymore, and her brother Oliver? He'd been useless from the get-go, relying on Chloe as his liaison. In theory, the decisions had come from Oliver but Chloe had been the show manager.

When Oliver had officially stepped away from

managing the rodeo earlier this year, Chloe hadn't hired anyone else to help run the show. She should have, though. She had to be drowning in work. They were a long way from Dallas and Chloe had no backup.

Managing the All-Stars was a full-time job and she'd also started that Princess clothing line. His sister, Marie, had bought a couple of shirts, ostensibly so she and Pete could make fun of the latest tacky venture from the tacky Lawrences. But Marie—the traitor—had actually liked the clothing so much she'd bought a few more pieces.

Chloe could have her little fashion show—Pete didn't care about that at all. But she was going to ruin his rodeo and he wasn't going to stand for that.

The contractors and local rodeo boards—they wanted to work with him, not her. Not Oliver Lawrence. And they'd never trusted New Yorker Milt Lawrence, with his fake Texas accent.

Pete could rally everyone who made the All-Stars work and get them to go on strike unless the Lawrence family either divested themselves of the circuit or paid Pete his fair share of the profits—going back thirteen long years. The rodeo was worth a lot of money—money that by rights belonged to the Wellington family.

But money wasn't why he was in Missouri this weekend. Between oil rights and cattle, his ranch was worth millions. No, this was about his father's legacy—about Pete's legacy. He wanted the All-Stars back.

So he'd proposed a solution to the stock contractors. The locals threatened to mutiny and, when things looked bleak, Pete would ride to the rescue, Chloe's knight in a shining Stetson. Chloe would be so grateful for his support that she would agree to Pete working for the All-Stars in one capacity or another. And once he was in, he'd slowly begin to crowd Chloe out.

It was a hell of a risky plan but he'd tried everything else. This would work. It *had* to. By this time next year, Chloe would be completely out of the picture and the All-Stars would be his.

Provided, of course, that Dustin Yardley didn't blow the plan to bits before it got off the ground.

Chloe swung back to him, her eyes narrowed. Suspicion rolled off her in waves. "Is there something you'd like to tell me, Pete?" She bit off each word as if it had personally offended her.

He had to make this look good. The plan would work fine even if she was a little suspicious of him, but he needed her to hire him on. Pete was walking a fine line and he knew it.

"Steve Mortimer gave me a call. He's under the weather and wasn't able to get his horses here, so he asked me if I could help out. I guess he must've asked Dustin first, but you know Dustin." That wasn't exactly how it'd happened. It'd cost Pete a pretty penny to get Steve to stay home this weekend. The man did love his rodeo. But then, so did they all.

Chloe gave him a hard look before her entire face changed. It was like watching a cloud scuttle past the sun because suddenly, everything was brighter. Yet, at the same time, that look irritated him. Like she'd flipped a damned switch, Chloe Lawrence looked instantly dumber. If Pete hadn't watched it happen, he might not have noticed the difference.

He'd say this for Chloe Lawrence—she was a hell of an actress.

She swung around to face Dustin. An inane giggle issued forth from her mouth. She was smart, Pete had to give her that. Dustin Yardley would never admit to being outmaneuvered by a girl.

"I'm so glad Mortimer trusted you enough to call you first," she said, her voice rising on the end as if she were asking a question.

Pete frowned at her. He understood what she was doing, but that didn't mean he had to like it.

Then again, when had she ever done anything he'd liked? He didn't like the way she ran the rodeo. He didn't like the changes she wanted to institute. He didn't like the way she used the rodeo to promote her own princess-ness.

The All-Stars wasn't about Chloe Lawrence. It didn't exist to sell clothing or stuffed animals or—God help him—Lawrence Oil, a subsidiary of Lawrence Energies, owned solely by the Lawrence family. The All-Around All-Stars existed for one reason and one reason only—to celebrate the best of the best of ranchers and cowboys. To take pride in ranching. To connect them to the tough men and women who had tamed the Wild West.

None of those things applied to Chloe Lawrence. She'd been born in New York, for God's sake.

Dustin looked confused. The man was mucking this up. Then, at the last possible second, Dustin got a grip on the situation. "Yeah, good old Steve. I, uh, didn't have any room, uh, in my trailer. For his horses. I was glad Pete was able to pick up the slack."

Yeah, *that* was believable.

"But that doesn't change anything else," Dustin went on, talking over Chloe's head to Pete. "It's not right to have women riding in our rodeo. They're distracting and they could get hurt. She's the god-damned Princess of the Rodeo. She shouldn't be making decisions like this, and God save us all from that arrogant ass of a brother of hers."

"Which one?" someone from the crowd asked.

"They're both asses," Dustin announced with grim satisfaction.

Pete watched the tension ripple down Chloe's shoulders and he knew without even looking at her face that she had lost her innocent mask and was about to tear Dustin a well-deserved new one. But before she could launch into her tirade, Pete stepped forward. "How about a compromise?"

"How about you go screw yourself?" Chloe said under her voice.

Pete damn near bit his tongue, trying not to laugh at that quiet jab. Never let it be said the woman didn't give as good as she got.

"Ms. Lawrence isn't wrong," he went on as if she hadn't just insulted him. "A rising tide does lift all boats. Making the All-Stars bigger will mean more money for you, for the riders and, yes, for management. And she's not wrong that having a woman ranked in the top ten in the Total Bull Challenge has brought in a lot more money to that outfit. Are you guys trying to tell me you would rather remain a second-tier rodeo organization rather than open up the All-Stars to new blood?"

Dustin glared at him, but that was to be expected. Pete was more concerned about what Mort and Dale and the riders would think. If other people bought into Dustin's way of thinking, Chloe would dig in her heels and the rift could tear the All-Stars apart. A flash of terror spiked through him. That was definitely *not* part of the plan. He wanted his rodeo back intact, thank you very much.

Chloe turned so she could look at Pete sideways. "Have you been replaced by aliens or something?" she asked in that same quiet voice, and oddly, he was reassured that she didn't sound inane or ditzy.

He wanted to deal with the real Chloe Lawrence. No tricks, no deceptions.

Which was ridiculous because he was actively engaging in deception as they spoke.

"Doesn't sound much like a compromise," Dustin grumbled.

"I'm getting to that." Pete put on a good grin, the kind he used in bars on Friday nights when a pretty girl caught his eye. "We all want to make more money and Chloe has a few interesting ideas that are taking a lot of her time and attention."

She kicked at the dirt. "A *few*?" But again, she was talking only to him.

He ignored her, knowing it would do nothing but piss her off. "Maybe it'd be best if we let her focus on high-level marketing and expansion stuff, the kind that will bring in new viewers and new fans, and leave the nitty-gritty details to someone who doesn't mind getting his hands dirty, someone people know and trust."

"We?" she challenged. Damn. Pete had been hoping that would slip right past her.

"Someone like you?" Dale said on cue. Thank God someone was hitting their marks today.

"I am going to kill you," she whispered even as her eyes lit up and she smiled as if this were a great idea. *"Slowly."*

He ducked his head as he stepped around her. "You can try," he whispered back, and then he turned his attention to the gentlemen gathered around him. "What do you all say? Does that sound like a workable solution? Chloe can keep doing her part to move the rodeo forward and I can handle everything else." He winked at the crowd where Chloe couldn't see it.

Dustin looked like he wanted to challenge someone to a gunfight, but Pete had most everyone else and that was the important part.

"Might not be a bad idea," Dale mused. "After all, we know and respect Pete."

Pete couldn't see Chloe's face, but he heard the sharp intake of breath at what wasn't said. Sure, they all knew and respected Pete—but they didn't respect her. It didn't matter how long she'd been riding at the All-Stars rodeos.

She would never really belong here. It was high time she realized that.

"Well," she managed to say in a voice that sounded relieved, if a little airheaded. "I'm so glad *we* were able to find a solution that works for everyone! And Mr. Wellington, I'm extra glad you are able to bring your horses all the way to the Bootheel." Her grin was so bright it about blinded him. "I'd like to remind everyone that showtime is in three hours and we do have a sold-out crowd tonight and an almost sold-out crowd tomorrow night. Let's give these people a reason to come back that doesn't involve funnel cakes."

She got a little bit of a laugh for this and she kept that big smile going, but Pete could see the light dying in her eyes a little bit.

Good. That's just what he wanted. He didn't feel the least bit sorry that she'd been overthrown in a mutiny. It was past time she found out what it was like to have a usurper sitting on the throne of one's inheritance.

Still… Watching her grit her teeth as she shook hands with cowboys bothered Pete a little bit. These men had been nothing but rude to her today. Some of them had dressed it up with prettier language than others, but still. She had to pretend like this was all hunky-dory because if she punched someone like her brother would've, they'd start in on how it was more proof that women shouldn't be in charge of these things.

That's just the way it went. What was done was done and the end justified the means. He had successfully accomplished the first step in taking back *his* rodeo and he couldn't afford to let things get personal. Nothing he felt for Chloe was personal and that was *final*.

She turned to him. "When you get time," she said, sweetness dripping off every word, "I'd like to go over your new duties with you."

Which meant she was going to try to destroy him. Pete grinned. He'd like to see her try. "Absolutely," he told her, fighting the odd urge to bow. "You're the boss."

Fire danced in her eyes, promising terrible, wonderful things. She tilted her head in acknowledgment of this false platitude and then sashayed off, her head held high and her hips swaying in a seductive rhythm. Pete knew he wasn't the only one watching the Princess of the Rodeo leave him in the dust. The woman was an eyeful.

Just as she got to the gate, she turned and looked back over her shoulder. Sunshine lit her from behind, framing her in a golden glow. Damn, she was picture-perfect, every fantasy he'd ever had come to life. If he didn't know who she was, he'd be beating these other idiots off with a stick to get to her first.

But he did know. She was an illusion, a mirage. She dressed the part, but she was nothing but a city slicker and interloper. A gorgeous, intelligent, driven interloper.

Their gazes collided and his pulse began to pound with something that felt an awful lot like lust. Even at this distance, he could feel the weight of her anger slicing through the air, hitting him midchest.

Oowee, if looks could kill, he'd be bleeding out in the dirt.

With a flip of her hair, she was gone.

"Well, how about that," Dale said, laughter in his voice. "You got your work cut out for you, Pete."

Oh, yeah, he was going to have his hands full, all right.

It was time to show Chloe Lawrence that the All-Stars was his. But she wasn't going to make this easy.

The thought made him smile. He was already starting to like this job.

Three

Chloe's hands were shaking as she sat at her make-shift makeup table in her makeshift dressing room. Which made applying her false eyelashes somewhat of a challenge. She forced herself to take a few deep breaths.

She was going to kill Pete Wellington. It wasn't a question of *if.* It was a question of *how.*

She'd love to run him down with her glossy palomino—but Wonder was at home, enjoying her hay and oats at Sunshine Ridge, Chloe's small ranch retreat northeast of Dallas. With all the things she had to juggle, she couldn't handle taking care of her horse, too. It wasn't fair to Wonder and it wasn't fair to Chloe. So she was borrowing a horse for her big entrance tonight.

Frankly, it didn't feel right running Pete down with a borrowed horse. Too many complications.

That man was up to something. If Steve Mortimer had had a problem getting his horses to the Bootheel, he would've called Chloe. It was obvious Mortimer had no such problems.

What kind of deal had Pete made with the stock contractors?

And how did backing her up when she was under siege figure into it? Because he wasn't doing it solely out of the kindness of his heart. This was Pete Wellington she was talking about—there was no kindness in his heart. Not for her or anyone in her family. She didn't want to offer him a job. She didn't want him anywhere near her. But...

If she didn't hand off some of the responsibilities to Pete, would people break their contractual obligations in protest? She could hire someone else but then she'd have the exact same problem—the people who made the rodeos work would balk at dealing with an outsider. By the time she found a workable solution, the All-Stars might very well die on the vine. And who would take the blame for that?

She would.

Maybe she could arrange a stampede. Watching Pete get pulverized would be immensely satisfying.

There. Her hands were steady. Who knew thinking of ways to off her nemesis would be so calming?

Now she applied the false lashes easily. She wore them for the shows because she was moving around the arena at a controlled canter. If she didn't have over-the-top makeup and hair—not to mention the sequins—people wouldn't be able to see any part of her. She'd be nothing but an indistinct blur.

And if there was one thing the Princess of the Rodeo wasn't, it was *indistinct*.

She was halfway through the second lashes when someone knocked on her dressing room door. If one could call this broom closet a dressing room, that was. Hopefully, that was Ginger, who sat on the local board of this rodeo. If anyone could talk some sense into those stubborn old mules, it'd be Ginger. She took no crap from anyone.

Chloe still had an hour and a half before show-time, but the gates were already open and she needed to be out in the crowd, posing for pictures and hand selling the Princess clothing line. She was behind schedule thanks to Pete Wellington, the jerk. She finished the lashes and said, "Come in."

Of course it wasn't Ginger. *Of course* it was Pete Wellington, poking his head around the door and then recoiling in shock.

"What do you want?" she asked, fighting the urge to drop her head in her hands. She didn't want to mess up her extravagant eye shadow, after all. Then she'd be even further behind schedule.

He was here for a reason. Was it the usual reason—he wanted his rodeo back? Or was there something else?

"I want you to put on some damned clothes," Pete said through the open door. At least he wasn't staring.

Chloe frowned at her reflection. "It's a sports bra, Pete. It's the same one I wear when I go jogging. The same basic style women across the country wear when they're working out."

It was a really good bra, too. Chloe had perfectly average breasts. And she'd come to a place in her life where she was happy with perfectly average breasts. She liked them. They were just right. Anything bigger would make cantering around arenas every weekend downright painful.

That didn't mean she hadn't gone out of her way to buy a high-end sports bra that provided plenty of padding. Everything about the Princess of the Rodeo was bigger, after all. She did a little shimmy, but nothing below her neck moved. She was locked and loaded in this thing and her boobs looked good. And completely covered. "It's not like you can see my nipples or anything."

"Dammit, Chloe, it's a *bra*," he growled back through the door. "I can't… You're… Look, just put on some clothes. *Please*."

Oh, she liked that note of desperation in his voice. Was it possible she'd misread the situation? For almost ten years now, she and Pete had been snarling at each other across arenas and in parking lots. She'd always thought her physical attributes had no impact on him because he'd never reacted to her before in that way.

But he was reacting now. She could hear the strain in his voice when he added, "Are you decent yet, woman?"

She stood, her reflection grinning back at her. "I don't know what you're complaining about," she said, plucking the heavily sequined white shirt off the hanger and sliding her arms through the sleeves. "I'd be willing to bet large sums of money you've seen your sister in a sports bra and never thought twice about it. And yes, I'm decent."

"Let's get one thing straight, Lawrence—you are *not* my..." Pete pushed his way into the dressing room, which was not designed to hold a man his size. The space between them—no more than a foot and half—sparked with heat as his gaze fell to her chest. "Sister," he finished, his voice coming out almost strangled as he stared at the open front of her shirt.

"Thank God for that," Chloe said lightly as she brushed her hands over the sequins—which conveniently lay over the sides of her breasts. "I pity Marie for having to put up with you, I really do."

She'd never had a problem with Marie Wellington, who worked her wife's ranch in western Texas. But then again, Marie had made it clear some years ago that she didn't care if the Wellingtons got control of the All-Stars or not. "It's just a rodeo," Marie had confided over a beer with Chloe one night. "I don't know why Pete can't let it go."

In the years since then, Chloe hadn't gotten any closer to finding out why, either. But if the man was going to torture her, she was going to return the favor—in spades.

Her hands reached the bottom of the shirt and she took her time making sure the hem was lined up.

Pete's mouth flopped open as Chloe closed the shirt, one button at a time. She probably could've asked him for the keys to his truck and he would've handed them over without even blinking. She had him completely stunned and that made him…vulnerable.

To her.

She let her fingers linger over that button right between her breasts as Pete began breathing harder, his eyes darkening. The cords of his neck began to bulge out and she had the wildest urge to lick her way up and down them. The space between them seemed to shrink, even though neither of them moved. Her skin heated as he stared, tension coiling low in her belly.

Crap, she'd miscalculated again. Did she have Pete Wellington at her mercy? Pretty much. But she hadn't accounted for the fact that desire could be a two-way street. He'd always been an intensely handsome man. She wasn't too proud to admit she'd had a crush on him for a couple years when she'd first started riding at the rodeos, until it became clear that he would never view her as anything more than an obstacle to regaining his rodeo.

But the way he was looking at her right now, naked lust in his eyes instead of sneering contempt?

He wanted her. And that?

That took everything handsome about him and made him almost unbearably gorgeous. Her pulse began to pound and, as she skimmed her fingers up her chest to ostensibly reach for the next button, she had to fight back a moan.

"There," she said as she fastened the last button,

and dammit, her voice came out breathy. "Is that decent enough for you?"

Pete's gaze lingered on her body for another two seconds before he wrenched his whole head up. His eyes were glazed. She probably couldn't have stunned him any better than if she'd hit him on the head with a two-by-four. Chloe had to bite her lower lip to keep from saying something wildly inappropriate, like *I'll undo all of those buttons while you watch* or maybe just a simple, effective *your turn*.

Talk about wildly inappropriate. Instead, she said, "What do you want?" because that was the question she needed the answer to.

His presence wasn't an accident and he was plotting something. But her words didn't come out as an accusation. At least, it didn't sound like one to her. It almost sounded like...an invitation.

He swallowed hard, his Adam's apple bobbing with the motion. The look in his eyes said one word and one word only—*you.* "We, uh, have to talk. About the job."

Right, right. The job. The rodeo. The feud between their families, going back over thirteen years. The way she knew he was here to undermine her but she wasn't sure how supporting her was going to help with that.

None of that had a damned thing to do with the way his eyes devoured her.

She turned and bent at the waist to check her makeup in the small travel mirror. Pete made a noise behind her that sounded suspiciously like a groan.

She glanced back at him in the reflection and saw that he was, predictably, staring at her behind. "Yes, the job. The one you volunteered yourself for?"

"Yeah." He swallowed again. "That job."

She reached over and picked up her chaps. They were show chaps, bright white leather that had never seen a speck of dirt or a spot of cow manure. With supple fringe at the edges, the chaps had "All-Stars" worked in beads running vertically down each of her thighs and then, at the widest part of the chaps at the bottom, "Princess of the Rodeo" had been spelled out in eye-popping gems of pink and silver. Nothing about these chaps were subtle and everything was designed to catch the eye. She always wore the white outfit on the first night of the rodeo. The second night, she had another matching outfit in patriotic red, white and blue. Those chaps were so covered with rhinestones she needed help mounting up in the saddle.

"What I'm trying to figure out," she said, propping one leg up on the chair and strapping the chap around her upper thigh, "is why you want the job, Pete. By all accounts, you don't need the money. I know Marie's ranch does well, too."

Chloe had done her research—he was quite well off. He wasn't at the same level the Lawrence family was, but his net worth meant he didn't *need* this job. Gorgeous, wealthy, rugged—Pete Wellington was a hell of a catch no matter how she looked at him.

And she was looking at him right now. He stared at her with naked desire and she could feel her traitorous body reacting. If it weren't for his hell-bent vendetta, she'd be tempted.

A shudder worked through her body as she went on, "And you haven't exactly shown a willingness to work beneath a woman in general or me in specific."

He had his thumbs hooked into his belt, but he was gripping the leather so hard his knuckles were white. She'd put a lot of money on the fact that he wouldn't be able to tell her what she'd just said.

But this man was just full of surprises, wasn't he? "I never said I have any problem working under you," he said in a low voice that made that tight coil of desire in her stomach painfully tighter. "In fact, I'm beginning to think it's a good idea to have you over me."

Her fingers fumbled with the strap and she had to stop before the heavy leather fell off her leg entirely. Her hands were shaking again, but this time it wasn't with rage.

Damn this man. Even when he pissed the hell out of her, he still had the capacity to make her want him. At least this time, she knew she'd made him want her, too.

It wasn't so much cold comfort as it was outright torture, however.

She took a deep breath, hoping to clear her head—but it didn't work because now his scent was filling this tiny space. Leather and dirt and musk. He smelled exactly like a cowboy should, rough and maybe a little dirty but so, *so* right.

"Good," she managed to get out, but she didn't

sound in charge by any stretch of the imagination. "I'm glad you're coming to your senses." There. She managed to get the straps on the first chap done and turned her attention to the second chap. Which required her to switch legs. She leaned into the mild stretch and this time, Pete definitely groaned.

She couldn't think of anything to say that wouldn't come out as "Could you help me with this?" and no matter how hot he was making her, she was absolutely not about to have sex with Pete Wellington in a glorified broom closet.

Or anywhere else, she mentally corrected.

Sex with Pete Wellington was completely off the table. Or any other flat surface. That was final.

So she kept her mouth shut as she worked at the buckle. When she had that one done, she belted the chaps at her waist, which finished the whole look off with the giant belt buckle that had *Princess* worked in Swarovski crystals. Her dad had commissioned it for her when she'd turned eighteen.

She turned back to the mirror, trying not to look at the man behind her, but it wasn't easy. He must've taken a step forward at some point because he loomed over her now. She could feel his breath messing up her carefully curled hair and it was tempting—so damned *tempting*—to lean back into that broad chest, just to see what he'd do. Would he push her hair to the side and press his lips against the little bit of skin right below her ear? Cup her breasts through the sequins? Run his hands down her waist and around to her denim-clad butt?

She physically shook as these thoughts tumbled through her mind. She never hooked up at any of the All-Stars events—which was both company policy and her own personal rule. Cowboys were off-limits. But she lived out of a suitcase seven months of the year, which didn't make it easy to have relationships, either.

It'd been too long since a man had gotten this close to her.

Why, oh why did it have to be Pete *freaking* Wellington? He might be turning her on and she might be driving him crazy, but a little raw sexual attraction didn't change anything. He wasn't here by accident and she couldn't give him any more leverage over her. For all she knew, this attraction was part of whatever con he was running. Get her in a compromising position and blackmail her or something.

She leaned forward and plucked her white Stetson out of its travel case. The hat had a fancy sparkling crown that matched her chaps. She carefully set it on her head, making sure not to disrupt the curls she'd teased into her hair. There. Now she was the Princess of the Rodeo.

"Chloe…" Pete spoke the moment before his hands came to rest around her waist.

Her breath caught in her throat at the feel of his strong hands touching her. Had they ever touched before?

Ten years they'd been dancing around each other, slinging insults and innuendos in a never-ending attempt to come out on top—but had they ever actually *touched*?

She didn't think so because she would've remembered the electric feel of his fingers on her body, the rush of heat that flowed out from this connection.

How would his rough, calloused hands feel against her bare skin?

"Yes?" Her gaze caught his in the mirror. She wanted to cover his hands with her own, lace their fingers together. She wanted to pull him closer.

She had lost her ever-loving mind.

But even that realization didn't make her move. She couldn't. She had to know what he was going to say. His mouth opened and she held her breath.

Bam bam bam. The crappy door to this closet practically bowed under the force of the pounding as Flash called out, "Chloe! You in there?"

Pete dropped his hands and backed up so fast he tripped over her rolling luggage and all but fell into the far corner of the tiny space. Chloe tried not to groan out loud. There was no situation her brother couldn't make worse. "Yeah, I'm almost ready." To Pete, she hissed, "Here's the deal, Wellington. I know whatever you're doing is a trap, but…"

"But?" he replied, almost—but not quite—pulling off a nonchalant look. He was breathing too hard to look casual about anything.

She didn't miss his lack of a denial. Right. Nothing like a confirmation that he was completely untrustworthy to help squash her rampant desire.

She took a deep breath, inhaling more of his scent,

and did something she'd sworn she'd never do. She admitted weakness to Pete Wellington. "But you're not wrong that I need a little help handling the stock contractors and the cowboys. Do you legitimately want to work with the All-Around All-Stars Rodeo?"

He had the nerve to look indignant. "Isn't that all I've ever wanted?"

"No," she whispered furiously. "You've always wanted to put me in my place."

"Did we determine if that was above me or below me?" he asked with a sly grin.

And just like that, they were right back to the same place they'd always been. She ignored his question. "I will tolerate your presence as long as you do what I say, when I say it. If you can convince the locals to get on board with my ideas, then you can stay. But the moment you undermine me, you're gone and I'll see to it you never set foot at an All-Stars event ever again. Understood?"

Flash banged on the door again. "Chloe? Is everything all right? I heard Pete Wellington is here. Do you know what that asshole wants?"

Irritating little brothers would always be irritating, even if they weren't little anymore. She had no idea if she was pissed at Flash or thankful that he'd interrupted the madness she and Pete had been barreling toward at top speed. "One second, for God's sake," she snapped. She jabbed a finger in Pete's direction, but she made sure not to touch him. "Understood?"

It took him a while before he responded. She

could practically see the lust fading away, replaced with his usual condescension. "Understood, *boss*."

"Can you handle leaving my dressing room without getting caught?"

He gave her a dull look. "Go before he breaks down the damned door."

She threw the door open—which conveniently slammed into Pete's chest. She gave him one last warning look and then had to dodge Flash's next knock as she quickly walked away from her dressing room. "What?"

Thank God Flash followed her. He already had his chaps belted on, but unlike hers, Flash's weren't all that flashy. Dirt and muck from the arenas he'd been riding in for the last six years had permanently worked into the creases. Chaps that had once been a light brown with a darker brown diamond pattern down the leg were now just…dirty brown. "Who's the act tomorrow night?"

"You had to interrupt me getting ready to ask me a question you could have looked up on the internet?"

She was *so* done with this day, honestly. She needed a stiff drink and maybe a video call with her sister-in-law, Renee Lawrence. She and Renee had been best friends back when Chloe had grown up in New York City, before Milt Lawrence had won the All-Stars in that ill-fated poker game and relocated his entire family to Dallas.

A few months ago, Renee had gotten into a little trouble—which was the nicest way anyone could say her husband had committed suicide rather than face charges for his part in what the newspapers had dubbed the Preston Pyramid, the largest financial con in American history. Renee had come to Dallas looking for Chloe but had found Oliver, the oldest of the Lawrence children and somehow, two people who had driven each other crazy as kids had absolutely clicked as adults. Now one of Chloe's oldest, dearest friends was her sister.

She could use some girl time, frankly, away from the overwhelming masculinity of the rodeo. Renee had no history with Pete Wellington either, so Chloe could work through her suddenly complicated feelings.

But instead she had Flash.

Her brother scratched the back of his neck. "Yeah, yeah, I know. I was just wondering…you know, if the act had changed."

Flash was many things—a cocky pain in the butt, mostly—but hesitant wasn't one of them. To see him hemming and hawing was unsettling, frankly. "What? Were you hoping to see someone else?"

"Never mind. Forget I said anything."

She stared at her brother. Why did she think this was about a woman? When it came to Flash Lawrence, he only cared about two things—women or earning his place at the All-Stars table.

Then it hit her. "Is this about Brooke Bonner?"

"No," he answered quickly, but his cheeks shot red.

"Uh-huh."

At the All-Stars rodeo in Fort Worth early in the

season, Brooke had been an up-and-coming country star. And it hadn't escaped Chloe's notice that Flash and Brooke had both disappeared about the same time after the rides and before Brooke's show. They'd had to delay the start of the concert for twenty minutes before Brooke had reappeared, claiming she'd gotten lost backstage.

If Chloe had the time or mental energy, she'd go for Flash's jugular over his country-star crush because the man had earned more than a little crap for all the times he'd made Chloe's life that much more complicated. But today, she didn't have it in her. She was late, still flustered from whatever the hell had happened between her and Pete and still furious that none of the stock contractors were willing to agree to her ideas until Pete declared them okay. So instead of ribbing her brother, she only said, "If there's any change in the music lineups, I'll let you know. Okay?"

"Okay, thanks." Her baby brother smiled at her, the good smile that drew buckle bunnies to him like moths to a flame. But underneath that cocky grin was relief.

"But," she went on, "you owe me." Before Flash could interrupt her, she went on, "Yes, Pete Wellington is here. And I've hired him—on a trial basis," she practically had to shout over Flash's holler of disbelief. "He's going to run interference with the stock contractors. I'm asking you as a sister and ordering you as your boss not to start anything with him. Okay?"

"Have you lost your ever-loving mind?" Flash demanded, scuffing the toe of his boot into the dirt. "You can't trust that man. He's out to take us all down."

"Who said I trusted him?" No, she didn't trust Pete at all. But aside from Flash, she was alone in that judgment. Everyone else here had made their feelings crystal clear—they'd pick Pete over her every day of the week.

She just needed a little help while she pushed the All-Stars through this transition phase, that was all. She'd make full use of Pete's ability to get cowboys to shut up and go along with the plan and then, when she had the All-Stars positioned properly, she'd cut him loose.

All there was to this…relationship with Pete Wellington was a calculated risk. He was betting he could trick her out of the rodeo, somehow. She was betting he was no match for her. He might be gorgeous, wealthy and awfully good with a rope, but she was a Lawrence.

Flash looked doubtful, so Chloe went on, "Look— trust me. I know what I'm doing and I know what he's trying to do—but I can handle him. Just don't pick a fight with him, okay?"

"If you need someone to run interference, why not just ask me?"

The hell of it was, Flash meant that. He hadn't seen the messes she'd had to clean up after all his other attempts to "help." Flash would always be a big bull in a very tiny china shop.

"Because," she explained, "you want to be a rider, not a Lawrence. You start meddling in the show management and no one will ever believe you've earned your ranking."

Flash was hell-bent on being one of the best all-around riders in the world, which meant riding with the All-Stars. But the problem with riding the rodeo circuit your family owned was that no one believed he hadn't just bought his way into the rankings. Everyone—even the competitors who watched him ride night after night—believed he was here only because he was a Lawrence.

"Fine," he grumbled. "You're right. But why does it have to be Pete?"

Chloe grit her teeth. "Because everyone else already respects him. They listen to him." And not to her.

She pushed that thought aside and went on, "If I bring in someone new, it'll take months—maybe years—before they're willing to try something different and I have plans, Flash. I want them in place before the next season starts." That was the one area where Pete had her up against a wall.

No, no—wrong mental image. Because Pete would never have her up against a wall.

But she needed his connections and goodwill *now*.

Flash scowled. "If Pete gives you any crap at all, I'll beat the hell out of him."

"Agreed," she said and then pasted on her big smile as a family with two little girls spotted them.

"Well, now—who are these two beautiful princesses?"

The girls squealed and hugged her and Chloe posed for pictures with the mom and her daughters and then, with surprisingly good humor, Flash posed with the dad.

By then, other people had noticed the Princess of the Rodeo and a crowd formed. As Chloe posed for another picture, she saw Pete Wellington in the distance, talking with a few of the riders. As if he could sense her gaze upon him, he turned. And tipped his hat in her direction.

Another thrill of pleasure went through her at the gentlemanly gesture. No, she didn't trust him. Not a damned bit. But it looked like they were working together from here on out.

This was a bad idea.

After what had almost happened in the dressing room? It was a horrible idea, one that almost guaranteed failure.

But as long as she kept her fantasies to herself and Pete's hands off her body, it'd be fine.

No problem, right?

Four

Pete watched the opening procession from the top of the bull chutes. God, he'd missed being up here. Chloe was, predictably, first in line. His gut tightened as he looked at the way she sat in the saddle and remembered the way she'd looked in nothing more than a pair of skin-tight jeans and a bra, for God's sake, acting as if that were the most normal thing in the world. To say nothing of the way her nimble fingers had worked at the buckles of those ostentatious chaps as she strapped them on over her long, lean thighs...

He cleared his throat and shifted his legs, trying to take the pressure off his groin as Chloe stood in her stirrups, her ass cupped by those chaps.

When she'd first started this princess crap, Pete

had been twenty-three. That he remembered clearly because his dad had stopped by for his birthday and…well, Pete wasn't proud of what he'd done. But he'd been twenty-three and pissed as hell that the Lawrences were making a mockery of his rodeo. He couldn't take out his anger on a cute teenager like Chloe and her dad would've pressed charges if Pete had punched him. Besides, it'd been Davey Wellington's fault that Pete had lost his whole world in one drunken bet.

Even now, the betrayal still burned. The All-Stars had been the one thing he'd shared with his father and yet, Davey Wellington had just drunkenly gambled it away like the circuit hadn't meant anything to him. Like…like all the time he and Pete had spent together at rodeos hadn't meant anything.

When Pete had come into his oil money, Dad had been sick, with just a few months left. Pete had sucked up his pride and made Milt Lawrence an offer to buy back the All-Stars so that Pete and Davey could have a chance to relive those happier times. Pete had been determined to make things right. He'd even offered to let Chloe keep riding as the Princess of the Rodeo, if it would've made her happy.

Only to have the old man laugh in his face and have security escort Pete out of the building. Then he'd promptly kicked Pete off the All-Stars circuit.

After that, it was *war*.

Pete looked at the arena, at the families having a good time. His gaze traveled back behind the chutes, where riders and cowgirls were all humming with energy for the competition and he felt it again—that sense of homecoming. This was where he belonged. All of this should've been Pete's. Now that Dad was gone, this should've been his family because rodeo was family.

Instead, it was Chloe's.

But not for much longer.

Chloe was announced and she kicked her horse into a gallop, an enormous American flag billowing above her head. Pete followed her with his gaze. He wasn't staring. Everyone was watching her circle around the arena at top speed, expertly guiding her borrowed mount through the curves.

Huh. He didn't remember her riding quite so well. It'd been a while since he'd been able to bring himself to watch this farce. The last time he'd suffered through Chloe riding had been…a few years ago. Four, maybe?

She looked good up there.

She'd looked good in that closet, too, buttoning her shirt over her breasts, her breath coming hard and fast when he'd stepped in behind her and rested his hands on her waist. If Flash hadn't interrupted them…

"Do you have any idea what I'm going to do to you if you screw with my sister?"

Speak of the devil. Pete refused to cede any space as Flash Lawrence squeezed in next to him at the top of the chute, his big black hat pulled low over his head. A nervous energy hummed off Flash, which made him a decent rider in the arena and a loose cannon out of it.

Pete gave it a second before he replied and he made damned sure to sound bored as he said, "I imagine you'll talk a big game, throw a few wild punches, then get drunk and stumble off with the first buckle bunny who catches your eye. As usual." He was speaking from personal experience with Flash. The kid had caught him by surprise one night and given him a hell of a black eye.

Of course, Pete had returned the favor. Anyone who was old enough to get drunk and start a fight was old enough to finish one—on the floor, if need be. Which was where Flash had wound up after Pete had started swinging. It hadn't been a fair fight—Pete had a solid ten years on the kid and at least forty pounds. But Flash had started that one.

Out of the corner of his eye, Pete saw Flash's shoulders rise and fall. Pete couldn't tell if that was a sigh of resignation or a man fighting to keep control. But then Flash tilted his head and looked at Pete from underneath the brim of his hat. "You just can't let the past go, can you?"

Irritation rubbed over Pete's skin. "Sure I can. I don't hold it against you that you jumped me at a honky-tonk, do I?"

Flash snorted. "Yeah, you're clearly over it." He shifted, angling his entire body toward Pete. "We both know you're not here because you've moved on, Wellington." His voice dropped as the music shifted and the local rodeo queen led the rest of the procession out. He was quiet until the music hit a crescendo. "You hurt my sister and you won't have to worry about a barroom brawl."

"That sounds like a threat, Lawrence." But Pete was almost impressed with the bravado the kid was pulling off. Chloe wasn't the only one who'd grown up, it seemed.

Flash cracked a grin but it didn't reach his eyes. Those were hard with something that looked a lot like hatred. Pete recognized that look all too well. "Of course not, Wellie."

Pete gritted his teeth but otherwise didn't react. No way in hell he'd let someone who willingly chose to go by *Flash* get under his skin for a stupid nickname.

Flash slapped him on the shoulder and leaned forward. "It's a promise," he whispered and damn if a chill of dread didn't race down Pete's back because Flash Lawrence was doing a hell of a good job at pulling off *menacing*. He moved to walk past Pete but paused and added, "We'll be watching." Then he was gone.

The national anthem began to play and Pete whipped off his hat as Flash's words echoed around his head. Had the kid caught wind of Pete slipping out of Chloe's dressing room? Or was he simply fulfilling his brotherly duty?

Didn't matter. Either way, Flash hadn't told Pete anything he didn't already know.

The Lawrences didn't trust Pete.

They'd have to be total idiots to do so and, sadly,

they weren't that stupid. But Pete knew that'd be the case going in. For his plan to work, he didn't need them to trust him.

He just needed a foot in the door and, for the time being, he had one.

He had to make the most of it because if he screwed this up, he'd never get his rodeo back.

The last of the crowd was filtering out under the starlit sky and the last chords of the last song were fading from the air when Chloe finally dragged her boots back to her dressing room, where Pete had been waiting for her for at least forty minutes. The sound from the concert back here had been distorted something awful, but he hadn't wanted to risk Chloe trying to give him the slip.

She was moving slow, her head down and any trace of the princess long gone. "Chloe."

She pulled up short. "Oh, it's you."

"Yup, still me," he agreed. For some reason, he wanted to grin at her.

"Are you going to follow me into my dressing room again?" Her bright show smile was nowhere to be seen. She looked worn out. The fancy rodeo queen–style dress she'd changed into for the concert was literally weighing her down. The long, sequined skirt glowed in the dim light. Even in near dark, the woman still managed to shine.

He'd never seen her look so…less than perky. He should enjoy the fact that she looked like a bull had run over her because it was just more proof that she couldn't handle running the All-Stars. Oddly, though, that wasn't the emotion that snuck up on him. Instead, he felt an odd urge to wrap his arm around her shoulder and kiss her.

On the forehead, that was. Nowhere else.

He cleared his throat. "Nope." To hell with it. He did grin. "Not unless you want me to."

She made a noise of disgust. "Don't make me shoot you." But she said it without animosity as she trudged past him.

He caught her by the arm. Despite the summer heat, her dress had long lacy sleeves. "I do need to talk to you."

She opened her mouth as if she wanted to argue with him, but then stared down to where he was touching her. "Do you promise not to barge in on me this time?"

Something in her voice kicked his pulse up a notch. Yeah, he was fully aware she'd been messing with him earlier, using her stunning body to distract him and he wasn't too proud to admit that it had almost worked.

Okay, it *had* worked.

But that teasing sensuality was gone now and she sounded soft and vulnerable and it absolutely shouldn't affect him because he didn't like Chloe Lawrence. He didn't want her and he certainly didn't care one whit for her.

He let his hand trail down her arm until his fingers brushed against hers. Then he leaned in so he could say, "I promise," close to her ear.

She inhaled sharply, but only said, "Wait for me," before she pulled free and disappeared into her private closet.

Pete kicked up a heel on the nearby fence and exchanged a few pleasantries with the remaining riders milling around backstage. The only people still here were either roadies tearing down the stage or riders hoping to get an autograph after the concert. Most everyone else had secured their animals and headed to the bars. The stock contractors were long gone.

Pete scratched the back of his neck and did his level best not to think of Chloe changing clothes. He failed.

When had she changed out of her button-up shirt and jeans into that formal dress for the concert? Was she still wearing that sports bra? Or had she slipped into something slinkier, maybe something lacy that matched the dress? Something that cupped her breasts like a lover's hands and...

Pete slammed the door on any thoughts about Chloe's breasts, clothed or otherwise. He was thinking about...the long night ahead of him. Yeah, that was it. He didn't technically have a place to sleep tonight because his plan had come together way too late to get a room in this small Missouri town. All the hotels were sold out and had been for weeks, if not months, so he'd be in his truck tonight.

He looked up at the night sky. Chloe probably had a room, complete with a nice big bed, all to herself. Would she go right to sleep or would she shower to wash off the dust first?

Dammit. It was fine if she flaunted her hot body in an attempt to throw him off his game. Her looks were just another weapon at her disposal and this was war. He expected nothing less. It was *not* fine if he let her succeed.

He wanted it in writing that he was the show manager. He'd already laid out a contingency plan if Chloe balked—he would skip the next rodeo in Terre Haute but he'd be back at the one in Little Rock. She might get rid of him once, but he wasn't going away.

He could do this. He could take back his rodeo a bit at a time and then…

And then what?

The door to her dressing room opened and there she was, almost unrecognizable. Gone were the big hair and the sparkly, over-the-top clothing. Her hair had been pulled back into a low tail and she had on flip-flops. Chloe wore a soft pair of black pants that fit her like a second skin and a loose tee that hung off one shoulder, revealing her bra strap. It was not the wide, white strap he'd gotten an eyeful of earlier, but something dark and, God help him, *lacy.*

"You're still here. Plotting, I presume?"

She said it in such an offhand way, as if it were common knowledge that he was out to undermine her and not a point of contention between them. And she said it without the least hint of drama. He was her problem and she was going to meet him head-on.

Was it possible he was starting to do the unthinkable? Was he starting to *respect* Chloe Lawrence?

God help him, he just might be.

"We didn't discuss terms earlier."

She adjusted a small duffel slung over one shoulder and tilted her head to the side. The mass of hair she'd bound back fell over one shoulder and he had to fight the urge to bury his hands in it.

"Earlier?" she asked. "Ah, yes—when you freaked out and then watched me get dressed. You're right, I don't remember much discussion happening then."

He might have underestimated this woman. "I don't think 'freaked out' is an appropriate—"

"Freaked. Out." Then the worst thing in the world happened. She smiled. Warmth bloomed in Pete's chest as the moonlight glinted off her mouth.

"Surprised," he corrected.

"Fine." She looked around and rolled her shoulders as if they were tight with tension. Pete had to clench his fists to keep from stepping behind her and rubbing his thumbs into her exposed skin. "This is probably a terrible idea."

"Which part? The part where I barged in on you? Or the part where you agreed to hire me?" It felt risky asking that, but hey—maybe being casual was the way to go. If she let down her guard…

"The part where I ask if you want to get something to eat."

"Now?" It was out of his mouth before he could stop it.

"Filled up on funnel cakes, did you?" He couldn't see it, but he swore he could hear her eyes roll. "Yes, *now.* I'm hungry. I'm tired. I'm not negotiating with you under cover of darkness, Pete."

He stepped into her and lifted the duffel from her shoulder. This close, the scent of her filled his nose. Something sweet, fruity maybe—but underneath that was the musk of a woman. She smelled good enough to eat. "What are you in the mood for?"

The air between them began to hum with tension. Chloe looked up at him, her face hidden in shadows and for one crazy second, he wanted her to say his name.

Hell.

"There's not much left open," she said and he might have been hearing things, but her words sounded breathless. "The bars…"

"Will have too many drunk cowboys and buckle bunnies." The thought of some young buck hitting on Chloe was enough to get his hackles up.

"I'm not eating fast food."

"I don't suppose there's a nice restaurant open this late, where I can buy you a good steak and a better bottle of wine?" A fancy candle-lit dinner with roses on the table and soft music in the background would…

Well, it'd be the wrong thing. She certainly didn't deserve to be wined and dined.

"First off, not this late. And second off, I'm not putting that dress back on." She pulled away from him. "As long as we're not at the same bar Flash is at, it'll be fine. And he likes Jeremy's better. So we'll go to Mike's and get a corner booth and I'm getting a bacon cheeseburger. Deal?" She started walking toward her truck, a sleek black Ram pickup with custom pink swirls along the side.

"I'll buy you a beer. To celebrate our new partnership."

She stopped so suddenly she almost stumbled and looked back over her shoulder. Even though he couldn't make out the details of her face, he could feel the distrust radiating off her. "Don't start celebrating just yet, Wellington."

Yeah, he'd definitely underestimated her.

It was going to be a hell of a ride.

Five

"I'll get us a table," Pete said, his breath caressing Chloe's ear as his hand rested briefly on the small of her back. Then he was gone, cutting through the drunken crowds with a grace she wasn't sure she'd appreciated before this exact moment in time.

She shook her head, trying to get her thoughts in order. Dinner at eleven thirty at night with Pete was a truly bad idea, capping off a day full of spectacularly bad ideas. Chloe was starving and exhausted and the last thing she should be doing was standing in a bar filled with All-Stars riders dancing to a bad band, waiting for Pete Wellington to…take *care* of her, for pity's sake.

She'd lost her mind. That was the only reasonable explanation. She was not operating on all cylinders and Pete was the kind of opponent who'd take full advantage of her at her weakest.

No way in hell was she drinking a beer around the man.

At least Flash wasn't here. She couldn't deal with the headaches a Flash-Pete brawl would bring. She just wanted her dinner and maybe a dance and…

No, wait—no dancing. Absolutely not. Not even if Pete asked. Because if he pulled her into his arms and two-stepped her around the dance floor, his arms around her waist…well, she might do something that would make all previous terrible decisions look positively well planned.

Damn that man.

He was not sweeping her off her feet and she was not being swept. This was all part of the same dance they always did around each other. He was just mounting a different sort of assault and she was doing her best to fend him off.

Wasn't she?

The noise was deafening and the bar was hot with the press of bodies. The rodeo was a huge deal in this small town, one of the biggest weekends in the entire year and it felt like half of Missouri was packed into this one bar. It wouldn't be any better at the other one, she knew.

Ugh, what a mistake. There was no way she could negotiate with Pete in here at any volume other than bellowing. It only got worse when he made his way back to her and shouted in her ear, "No place to sit."

She sagged into him a bit but then he yelled, "I

found a waitress. If you don't mind, we can order to go and eat on the tailgate…"

Mind? Hell no, she didn't mind. What she minded was that Pete had not only come to the same conclusions she had, but had already found a workable solution that bordered on thoughtfulness.

She nodded.

"Bacon cheeseburger, right?"

Oh, Lord, she couldn't handle thoughtfulness, not from Pete Wellington. Not without some more sleep and distance between their bodies. "Double bacon cheeseburger and onion rings," she yelled back.

"Beer?"

"No."

He winked at her—a disturbing trend—and then disappeared into the crowd.

Chloe slipped out the door and instantly the volume ringing in her ears dropped to a manageable level. A breeze blew through, carrying away the smell of sweaty bodies and spilled beer.

Where had this day gone wrong? Oh, right—a bunch of sexist old men who might have been working with Pete. She had to remember that part.

So what was Pete trying to accomplish with all this thoughtfulness?

The same thing he was always trying to accomplish—getting his rodeo back. She didn't have any question about that. But she had to admire that he was going about it in a new way.

So he was trying to steal the All-Stars. Again. Reasoning with him had never worked before. How many times had she pointed out that it'd never really been his rodeo in the first place—it'd been his father's? He was not a fan of that logic.

So why was he turning on the charm now? Because he was and, heaven help her, she was in danger of being charmed.

Unless she missed her mark, he had one of two plans. Either he was going to push her out from the inside or...

A shiver ran down her back. Or he'd decided he could win her and get the rodeo all at once.

Sneaky. Very sneaky. The only problem with that second plan was that she wasn't anyone's prize to be won. Especially not his.

The door to Mike's swung open, bringing a blast of noise and heat. "Hey—" she started to say.

And pulled up short because it wasn't Pete.

Two men she'd never seen before all but fell out of the bar, giggling like schoolgirls. By the looks of their hats and T-shirts with the sleeves carefully torn off, she'd guess they were local boys out having a wild night.

They stumbled to a stop, holding each other up as they looked Chloe over with leering gazes. "Well, hellooo, nurse!" said the taller one, which made the shorter, beefier one giggle again.

She notched an eyebrow at the men and dropped back into a fighting stance. Bless her brothers for teaching her how to throw a punch. During her childhood in New York City, her mother and her nanny had shuttled Chloe to dance and gymnastics and music—all the standard classes for a girl of her social circle. Most of the time, Trixie Lawrence had also arranged shuttling for Renee Preston to the same classes. The two girls had been inseparable.

But when Chloe had started riding as the Princess of the Rodeo, her brothers had decided she should know how to throw a punch. And since it'd been one of those rare times when Oliver and Flash had agreed on something and since her father hadn't been in a big rush to get her back into dance classes, Chloe had gone along with it.

Thank God for that.

"Not interested," she said casually even as she slid to the side, putting more space between her and the men while also making sure she had room to run if she needed. A good punch was a great thing, but if two guys got her pinned against the wall, the odds weren't in her favor.

"Ooh, lookie here," the shorter one said, leering drunkenly at her. "And I thought all the pretty girls were inside."

Hell, the odds already weren't in her favor. Outnumbered and outweighed—and these guys were drunk. Should she kick off her flip-flops? She knew she should have packed her sneakers, dammit. *"Not. Interested."*

"Waiting for us, honey?" the taller one added, stepping toward her. The shorter one almost tipped over without his support.

Why didn't men ever listen? Because they never did. How were these guys any different from Dustin

Yardley refusing to try something just because a girl had suggested it? Or from Pete refusing to acknowledge that the damned All-Stars wasn't his?

"No means no," she said, shifting her weight and letting her fist fly as the tall guy made a clumsy grab at her. She couldn't deck Pete or Dustin or any of the other men who treated her as nothing but a pretty face, but by God she wasn't going to let this jerk assault her.

Her fist connected with a sickening-yet-satisfying crunch. Pain blossomed along her knuckles, making her gasp. But it was a good, solid punch. She hit him hard enough that he spun around, knocking back into his friend. The pair of them staggered until they landed in a heap next to the door.

"Why you little—" the one not bleeding said as the taller one made a muffled screaming noise.

"Leave me alone," she snarled, shifting her position again. Damn, her hand hurt. If she'd broken something, it'd be impossible to ride and carry the flag tomorrow night.

This was exactly why she never went out to the bars anymore. But the nice thing about anger was the adrenaline that came with it. Her hand stopped throbbing as the shorter guy threw off his buddy—still moaning—and scrambled awkwardly to his feet.

She couldn't throw another punch with the same hand, so she shifted again. She'd either get this one on an uppercut or she could try a well-placed kick, if she had the room to—

The door to the bar swung open and Pete came out. "They were out of onion...*hell*."

"Little help here?" Chloe said, trying to keep her voice calm. She didn't dare take her eyes off the guy on his feet.

"She bwoke my node!" howled the tall one. He'd made it to his knees, but blood was gushing down his face.

"Good." Pete cut past the one still on his feet. The shorter guy swayed, his fists up. "What the hell are *you* doing?" he demanded.

"Getting their asses kicked," Chloe muttered.

"Shut it," Pete snapped, thrusting the food back at her. Then he turned his attention to the men. "You've got five seconds to get the hell away from her."

The shorter one blinked before his hands fell to his side. "Sorry, dude—didn't know she was yours."

Oh, that just absolutely did it. "What the hell did you just say?" she shouted and suddenly Pete had her around the waist and was holding her back.

"Five," Pete growled. "Four. Then I'm letting her kick your ass while I laugh at you."

"Not worth the trouble," the shorter one muttered as he hefted his friend up.

Oh, she was going to show them trouble. "I'm gonna..."

"Chloe, stop," Pete hissed in her ear. Then he said, louder, "Three..."

"We're going, we're going. Come on, Jack."

"My *node*!" Jack howled.

"Two," Pete all but yelled, but the guys were

already shuffling off into the dark, bouncing off parked cars and trucks and occasionally yelling insults over their shoulders.

Chloe twisted out of his grasp. "Do you have any idea how infuriating that is?" she yelled.

Pete backed up, his hands raised in the universal sign of surrender. "Easy, honey."

"I am *so* not your honey and you know it. I told them I wasn't interested. I told them to leave me alone and what do they do? Make a grab at me. All you had to do was show up and be a man and suddenly, there they go," she shouted, waving in the direction they had stumbled.

"...Be a man?" he asked, his confusion obvious.

She wanted to throw something. She'd already punched something and in all honesty, it hadn't helped. "Yes! Do you have any idea what that's like?"

"Being a man?"

"Of course you don't! Because you're a man!"

Pete stared at her as if a small alien had landed on her forehead. She groaned. Of course he didn't understand. He was probably enjoying the hell out of her emotional reaction—another thing he could throw back in her face to prove she wasn't capable of running the All-Stars.

Suddenly, she was tired. She looked down, trying to get her thoughts in order as the adrenaline burned away.

Oh. She'd dropped their dinner on the ground. Her eyes began to burn. "I... I'm sorry."

Pete stepped in front of her. "Chloe," he said

softly, his hands resting on her shoulders. He gave her a little squeeze and she almost sank into him. "What on God's green earth are you apologizing for?"

"I dropped our food." She managed not to sniff, but it was a close thing. "And I lost my temper."

"And here I thought Flash had the short fuse in your family." His thumbs stroked over her shoulders and he made a low humming noise in the back of his throat. "Are you okay?"

No, not really. Her hand ached so much she could almost hear a high whine in her ears, and nothing had gone right today and she was so pitiful that she was on the verge of asking Pete Wellington, of all people, for a stinking hug.

Worst. Day. *Ever.*

"I'm fine," she said, trying to pull herself together because she couldn't give this man one more bullet to use as ammunition against her. She forced her head up, forced herself to meet Pete's gaze. "Why?"

"Why?" His lips quirked into a smile. "Oh, no reason." As he spoke, his hands drifted down her shoulders and then her arms until he lifted her hands and tilted them toward the street lamp. "Just that you broke the nose of an idiot who had a solid seven inches and sixty pounds on you."

"Seventy," she corrected. This time, she did sniff.

And then froze. Pete's gaze locked with hers as he lifted her bruised knuckles to his mouth and pressed his lips to her skin.

Heat flashed down her back and her knees weakened so fast that she staggered a little. Pete's arm was around her waist in a heartbeat even as he held on to her swollen hand. "Seventy, easy," he agreed as he supported her weight.

Which, of course, brought her chest flush with his. She wasn't strong enough, dammit. She just wasn't. Not after the day from hell, not after this man had come to her defense twice in one day. Yeah, it was a trap and a trick and a long con, but he was also thoughtful and charming and it was so damned nice not to have to fight another battle.

She didn't want to fight with him.

"Here's what we're going to do," he murmured, staring down into her eyes.

"What?" She couldn't even care that she sounded breathless as her nipples went hard.

He let go of her waist and her hand at the same time and she almost cried at the loss until, unexpectedly, he bent down and swept her off her feet.

Who knew Pete Wellington could be so bloody charming?

"I'm going to get you set up on the tailgate of my truck because my truck is farther from the front door, which means fewer idiots will be by to harass you." As he spoke, he carried her as if she was as light as a feather. "Then I'm going to get you dinner and a bag of ice for your hand."

"Ice would be great," she admitted, draping her arms around his neck and leaning her head against his shoulder. She shouldn't, but what the hell.

He wasn't lying, his truck was a heck of a lot farther away from the bar than hers. "Can I tell you something, if you promise you won't overreact?"

"Really?"

He looked down at her without breaking stride, that quirky smile still in place. "Just don't punch me, Lawrence. I've seen the damage you can do."

Was that a compliment? "Fine. No punching. What?"

They finally reached his truck and he set her down so he could lower the tailgate. It was a really nice truck, top-of-the-line Ford Super Duty. "What happened to that old piece of crap truck you used to drive?" she asked. "The one that was half-rusted away?" She went to hop up, but she couldn't put her weight on her punching hand and hissed in pain.

He *tsked* and stepped in front of her. Before she could brace herself, Pete put his hands on her waist. Again, that delicious heat flashed over her skin. "The rust bucket? That's been gone a long time, hon. I've come up in the world."

She looked up at Pete as his grip around her waist tightened. This was where they'd been earlier today, before Flash had started banging on the door.

Flash wasn't here this time. "Clearly," she teased. "That's why you want to work for the All-Stars. Because you need the money."

But instead of coming back firing, he just stared down at her. "That's not why."

"Then why, Pete?" Her voice had gotten softer but then again, he'd gotten closer.

He didn't answer for a long time. Then, his mouth

cocked into that half grin, he said, "You are, hands down, one of the most impressive women I've ever known," and the hell of it was he seemed completely sincere.

Before Chloe could react, he lifted her up and set her on the tailgate. Her eyes—and her mouth—were almost level with his now.

Not kissing Pete. No matter how good the compliments were.

"I bet you say that to all the girls who could break your nose with one punch," she managed to get out, but she couldn't bring herself to pull away.

"Nope. Just you."

Then he leaned forward and, despite all her resolve, her eyes fluttered closed in anticipation and one word floated through her mind—*finally*.

But instead of feeling his lips against hers, he kissed her on the forehead. Which was good. Great, even. It was sweet and it didn't presume anything and she was absolutely *not* disappointed.

Pete pulled away and headed back to the bar. "Stay here and try not to get into any more fights."

"They started it!" she called after him.

He stopped and looked at her over his shoulder. "But you finished it like a *boss*."

There was no mistaking the approval in his voice, warm and sweet.

Oh, heavens.

Was she starting to like Pete Wellington?

What else could go wrong today?

Six

As soon as Pete was sure Chloe couldn't see him, he took off at a dead run. If those assholes decided to double back, he had to get to them before they got to Chloe.

She might throw a hell of a punch against one drunk, but two would overwhelm her and if something happened…

He ran as fast as he could, weaving in and out of cars and trucks parked haphazardly around the bar. Finally, he found the idiots in question by a rusted-out Ford truck. The one with the busted nose was on his hands and knees, heaving up his guts, while the one who'd called Chloe rude names was sitting behind the wheel with his legs hanging out the door.

Man, Pete was tempted to go over there and finish

what Chloe had started. They'd scared the hell out of her. No, she hadn't exactly admitted that, but Pete wasn't some clueless greenhorn. She'd been terrified. But her fear had been buried under anger.

For once, he was thankful for the Lawrence temper. Never thought he'd live to see the day.

It wouldn't take him long to dispose of these two—a couple of quick punches to make sure these guys stayed down for the rest of the night. But then... there might be witnesses and, knowing Chloe, she'd notice if he got blood on his shirt and then she'd tear into him again about how he was a *man*, as if that were a crime or something.

He needed to get back to her. So, after one final look to make sure the guys weren't going anywhere, he made his way to the bar.

What had she meant by that, anyway? Of course he was a man. He'd never had any question about who he was.

Their dinner was exactly where Chloe had dropped it. Pete checked the bags. The containers were dinged up and some fries had escaped, but it all still looked edible. He gathered everything up and then, rather than fighting his way through the crowd, he cut around to the back door and stuck his head into the kitchen. "Hey, can I get some ice? Please?"

The staff was none too pleased to be taking orders through the back door and they had no problem letting him know it, but every moment he stood here begging for ice was another moment Chloe was alone in his truck. He needed to get back to her.

He'd almost kissed her.

Hell, he had kissed her, but not where he'd wanted to. And as he'd touched her skin with his lips, he'd inhaled her scent. That close up, he'd been able to figure out what the fruity smell was—green apples. She'd smelled good enough to eat and he'd be lying if he said he wasn't tempted.

But he was stronger than temptation.

Kissing Chloe might be a nice fringe benefit in the moment, but it was not a part of his larger plans. Knowing how she thought, kissing her would most likely take his careful planning and throw it right out the window. Then where would he be?

Still on the outside, watching city slickers exploit his rodeo.

Finally, he got a grocery bag full of ice, although it was more thrown at his head than handed to him. He thanked the staff and hurried back to Chloe.

He slowed down once he had her in his sights. She'd scooted to one side and had one elbow resting on the edge of the truck bed, her chin resting on her forearm as she stared up at the night sky. Sweet merciful heavens, she looked like every girl in every country song and he had a wild impulse to drive off into the night until they found a quiet field and could curl up in the bed of his truck, watching the stars.

He shook his head to clear that vision away.

"It's me," he announced. Sneaking up on her tonight was a bad idea. "Any trouble?"

"No. It was as quiet as it gets this close to a bar." She sat up and took the ice from him. "Oh, that feels so good," she all but moaned as she covered her sore knuckles.

His body tightened at her words. And that was just for ice. How would she sound if he put his hands on her body? If he buried himself inside of her?

Focus, Pete.

"Here, wait." He opened the truck door and dug into his glove box, finally finding a clean bandanna. "Let me wrap that so you don't freeze your skin." She held her hand steady as he looped the bandanna over her knuckles. "Did you break anything, do you think?"

She shook her head as he got the ice situated. "It's sore, but everything moves like it's supposed to. Going to be hard to carry that flag tomorrow, though."

"If anyone could do it, it'd be you." He handed her the container with her burger and then hopped up next to her, putting the rest of the food between them. It seemed safer that way. "If you lost any fries, they're still in the bag. They look okay, just a little squashed." This felt wrong. She deserved so much more than greasy bar food.

"Thanks."

"Tell me about your plans for the All-Stars," he said after a few minutes had passed. "You really want to open up the events to women competitors?"

"Oh, yeah," she replied around a mouthful of fries. "I've analyzed the stats and the revenue streams from the Total Bull Challenge since June Spotted Elk made the circuit and, between the marketing aimed at new, mostly female viewers and the network distribution deals, she's responsible for a solid 15 percent bump in profits. Some people argue with that—but you can't tell me that the numbers are a coincidence."

"Huh," he said, mostly because he'd never figured Chloe would analyze revenue streams, much less stats.

"I'd love to find a breakout star like that," she went on. "Tex McGraw has a natural grasp of branding—have you seen his Instagram page?"

"I'm not real big on social media," he admitted. Which was to say, he wasn't on it at all. His mom had tried to get him to join Facebook but his sister, Marie, had shown him what sorts of things Mom put out there and, well, ignorance was bliss.

"Shocking," she teased. "Take my word for it—with a solid marketing push from the All-Stars at a corporate level, we could get Tex some major sponsorships deals and get the All-Stars name out there."

Pete had to swallow his surprise with his burger. "You'd rather promote Tex than your own *brother*?"

"Hell, yeah," she scoffed. "This is the All-Stars, not the Lawrence Family Hour. Besides, it doesn't have to be Tex—although he's laid down a great platform. I'd love to get June to ride in a few events—she grew up on a ranch and can rope calves with the best of them. Even if it's just for an exhibition, it'd bring in viewers and we could cross promote with her fans, let them know the All-Stars exists—that sort of thing. But someone like Tex, where we can control the narrative and build a storyline over a season—yeah," she finished with a wistful sigh. "That'd be amazing. And then there's the title of Princess…"

Pete snorted before he could help it. "What, going to promote yourself to Queen of the Rodeo now?"

She gave him a dull look that made him smile. "Seriously? I'm not a teenager anymore and it's a little ridiculous that I'm still doing it after a decade, don't you think?"

Pete felt like she'd punched him right in the gut. Was he supposed to agree with her? Because he did, but saying so felt like a trap.

Luckily, she kept talking. "What I'd like to do is open up the title to other girls—which, again, would only grow our audience. Maybe a national scholarship competition with a year's reign or… I don't know, exactly. But it's time to shake things up. Besides," she added, jabbing a fry in his direction, "I'm tired of men barging in on me while I change. I'd rather just run the show."

Now what the hell was he supposed to say to that? He'd been operating under the assumption that Chloe *lived* to be the princess. He'd thought she was clinging to her moment of glory like barnacles to the hull of a ship. And…

And that she didn't care about the All-Stars beyond her moment in the spotlight.

Had he misread the situation? Had he misunderstood *her*? Because suddenly, he wasn't entirely sure who he was sitting next to. It certainly wasn't the same clueless city slicker he'd first laid eyes on ten years ago, barely able to stay in the saddle without dropping the flag.

He didn't like not knowing because he had a plan that was built on a set of undisputed facts, the most important of which was that Chloe Lawrence was an airheaded attention hog who was ruining his rodeo.

He felt dizzy, almost.

"Big ideas" was all he managed to say. Huge changes, really. But if they worked—and it sounded like she'd done the research—then it could be good for the rodeo.

"Yeah. But the old timers are going to fight me every step of the way, no doubt. Like they're afraid of girl cooties instead of seeing long-term growth as a positive. They'd rather stagnate and die of obsolescence, I guess."

He snorted. They fell silent as they finished eating, but his mind was spinning the whole time.

Chloe Lawrence was hell-bent on remaking the All-Stars into something different. No wonder Dustin Yardley and the others had been so mad this morning. The rodeo was about tradition and honor and legacy and, okay, maybe it was a bastion of male pride. What Chloe was talking about flew in the face of a lot of that.

But…she also had a point about stagnation. He didn't want the All-Stars to shrivel and die. He loved the rodeo and had ever since his dad had started the circuit back in the eighties. Pete's childhood had revolved around the All-Stars. It'd been the one time when his dad was around and interested and focused on Pete. Because Davey Wellington had never been focused on anything, including his family. Mom liked to say that if they'd known what attention deficit disorder was back when Dad was a kid, he'd have been the poster child for it.

Mom made the ranch profitable, all while getting dinner on the table. Dad had a nasty habit of getting distracted with bright, shiny ideas. Which could be good, like when he'd decided to start the All-Stars. But it could also be bad, like when he bet the rodeo in a poker game and lost. And now it was too late. Dad was gone.

But Pete could still honor the man's life and keep those special memories alive by taking control of his rodeo. But if the All-Stars lost riders to bull riding or other outfits and went into decline, where would that leave his legacy?

He was going to need a drink to deal with that answer. Several drinks.

He decided it was safer to change the subject. Chloe was flat out inhaling her food—which was all the more impressive, considering she was doing so one-handed. "You were hungry, weren't you?"

"I never eat before a show. It used to be because I got so nervous but now I'm just too busy. I try to eat a big breakfast but by this time of night…" She shrugged. "Man, that's a good burger."

"It'd be better with a beer."

"True." She sounded wistful about it. "But there's no way in hell I'm going to drink around you, Pete."

"Why not?" He was real proud that he managed

to keep any hurt he might or might not have felt at that sideswipe out of his voice. "I'd never go after you like those idiots tried to. You know that."

She turned and gave him a long look—such a long look, in fact, he began to squirm. He hid it behind scrounging for fries in the bag.

"That begs the question, doesn't it?"

She was setting him up for something but damned if he could see where this was going. Was she about to remind him he was a man again? "What question?"

"How *would* you go after me?"

He almost choked on a fry. So much for changing the subject to something safer. "Pardon?"

There was no way she meant that question in a sexual sense and it definitely wasn't a come-on. Even if he'd like it to be.

She set her empty container aside and swung around, crossing one leg over the other and leaning back against the side of the truck. With the ice and her wounded hand in her lap, she stared at him. "How *are* you going after me? Like, right now? Because we've danced around each other for a decade, Pete. Ten years of push and pull and not once—not *once*—have you ever been nice to me, much less defended me twice in one day."

He was thankful it was dark because his cheeks got hot with something that felt like shame and he'd rather take a punch than let Chloe Lawrence see him blush.

"And don't you dare try to pass it off as if you

haven't been *that* bad or *that* mean because I'm not in the mood for bull tonight, Pete."

"How about tomorrow? We could have this talk tomorrow."

Light from the street lamp across the way shone off her smile. "I've recently discovered that my tolerance for BS has lowered significantly. Why are you here, Pete? Why are you defending me? Why, after all this time, are you treating me like a person? Like—" she swallowed but didn't look away "—like a friend?"

Man, it was tempting to protest his innocence. The phrase *you never could take a joke* danced right up to the tip of his tongue before he bit it back.

She was right. Trying to blow off all the ways he'd attacked and undermined the Lawrence family and their management of the All-Stars over the years would be complete BS. Because he'd thrown everything he had at them—including but not limited to lawsuits—and nothing had worked.

But what was he supposed to say now? She knew why he was here and he knew why he was here. But he couldn't come right out with the truth, not before he and Chloe had the terms of his new position in writing.

"Maybe things changed. Maybe…" He said something that was supposed to be a bald-faced lie. "Maybe I changed."

Funny how that felt a lot like the truth.

But it wasn't, not really. The Lawrence family still owned the All-Stars and Pete wouldn't stop until he got it back. Chloe was just an obstacle Pete had to work around.

He looked at his obstacle. She was watching him from under her lashes and Pete had the sinking feeling she could tell what color his cheeks were.

"It won't work, you know."

"What won't?"

"Don't play dumb, Wellington," she scoffed. "It's beneath you and it's beneath me. This scheme you're working on—it won't work. You're only here for one reason. You want your rodeo back."

What he wanted was to lean forward and kiss her. Not just because he wanted to get her to stop talking— although he did. He wanted to know if things really had changed between them or if it was all just smoke and noise, like the fireworks they set off at the start of every rodeo.

He looked out at the night sky. The bar wasn't too far away from the highway but, aside from people coming and going from the bar, the rest of the street was quiet, with only the occasional semi rumbling over the overpass.

"Did it ever occur to you that you've won?" he heard himself say. "That you're right?"

"There, was that so hard?" She spoke softly, but he could hear the amusement in her voice.

He shot a hard look at her. "You've got a hell of a mouth on you, Chloe Lawrence."

It wasn't right, how much he liked that grin on her. "Don't change the subject. You were telling me I was right?"

"Yeah." He swallowed and had to look away. These words, they weren't the reason he was here but...did that make them any less honest? "It's been ten years and nothing's changed. I'm never going to pry the All-Stars away from your family. God knows I've tried everything, but you people are worse than deer ticks during a wet spring."

"There's the Pete Wellington I know," she muttered, but at least she didn't sound like she was going to punch him when she said it.

"I can either keep beating my head against the same brick wall that is Chloe Lawrence and her irritating brothers or..."

"Or you can get hired on to run the rodeo?" Yeah, she wasn't buying this.

But was he lying, really?

The darkness of midnight in Missouri blurred the hard edges around them, making buildings indistinct lumps on the landscape and he wasn't sure where one parked car ended and the next began. "The All-Stars is *everything* to me and I'm never going to get it back. I've lost more than one lawsuit and you won't sell. I'm running out of options."

That was the unvarnished truth and it hurt to admit it.

"So I can either cut my losses and walk away from the one thing I love in this life or I can suck up my pride and ask you to hire me on as a show manager. I won't try to undermine your authority, and I can keep doing the only thing I love—running the rodeo my father started."

He looked back at her. Had she bought that last bit? Because, yeah, some of that was the truth. But the part about not working against her was the mother of all whoppers.

She sat forward, her head tilted to one side as she studied him. Could she see where the truth ended and the lies began? Or had the darkness obscured the difference?

Chloe shook her head and swung her legs off the back of the truck. "And I'm supposed to believe that a man whose middle name might as well be Grudge is just going to turn over a new leaf and work under me?" She hopped down, cradling her hand, and began to walk away. "That you've decided my family hasn't ruined your life after all?"

He scrambled after her and caught her by the arm, spinning her around to face him. "Chloe, stop."

"I don't buy it, Pete," she said, her brows furrowed as she stared up at him. But she didn't pull away from him, so that was something. "It's a great story, a real heartbreaker. It'd make a hell of a country song but you're asking me to believe that you're going to back me up when I want to do things differently in your beloved rodeo? Because you've *changed*?"

"Yeah," he said, his tone gruff as he lowered his head to hers. "Yeah, I am."

Kissing Chloe Lawrence was not part of the plan but was that stopping him as he brushed his lips over hers? No, it wasn't.

Because he was kissing her anyway, dammit.

Not the rodeo, not the princess—her, Chloe with the smart mouth and the right hook and it felt so *right*.

She sighed into him, one arm going around his neck as the ice bag landed on his boot with a *thud*. He didn't care because Chloe opened her mouth for him and Pete got a little taste of heaven when her tongue tested the crease of his lips.

Holy hell, this woman. Why hadn't he kissed her before this? He could have been doing this for years!

He groaned, pulling her into his arms as he took what she gave and came back to ask for more. Greedily, he drank her in, shifting until he had her backed against the side of the truck. "Chloe," he whispered against her skin as he trailed his mouth down her neck. "God, Chloe."

She knocked his hat off his head and dug the fingers of her good hand into his hair. "Don't talk," she said, sounding almost angry about it. But then she lifted his hand to her breast and even the touch of her chilled skin wasn't enough to cool him off. "Just don't talk, Pete."

"Yes, ma'am." But that was the last bit of thinking he was capable of as his fingers closed around her breast. The warm weight filled his palm and he moaned at the feeling of her nipple going tight between his fingers. He went rock hard in an instant and suddenly, he needed more.

He needed everything. From her.

"Yeah," she breathed, which was all the encouragement Pete needed. He shoved his knee between her legs and ground his thigh against her sex. She gasped and bore down on him.

Her heat surrounded him and he grunted, shifting back and forth while she rode his leg. She threw her head back, which seemed like the perfect time to explore her breasts. He had to keep one hand braced on the truck so he didn't lose his balance, but he slipped the other one under her loose tee and cupped her breast again, teasing her nipple through the thin fabric.

"Lace," he murmured as he tugged the bra cup down and finally, *finally* got a handful of nothing but Chloe. "I wondered."

"Shut up and kiss me," she growled, pulling his mouth down to hers and kissing him with such raw desire that he almost lost control right then.

He couldn't let her unman him—at least, not without returning the favor. So he kissed her back as he stroked her breast and tormented her nipple and swallowed the noises she made because he couldn't bear for a single one of her gasps and moans to escape.

She broke the kiss to thrash her head from side to side, her weight heavy on his leg. She was close, he realized.

He jerked her loose tee to the side and lifted her breast to his mouth, sucking hard on her tight nipple. Once he had her firmly in his mouth, he used his free hand to reach down between her legs and rub until he found the spot that made her back arch into him.

"Come for me," he growled against her, pressing

hard against that spot as he scraped his teeth over her skin.

For once, Chloe Lawrence—the woman who'd *never* listened to him—did as she was told. With a shudder that was so hard she almost knocked him off his feet, she came apart in his arms. Pete looked up just in time to see her face as the climax hit its peak.

Jesus, she took his breath away. Had he ever seen a woman as beautiful, as vulnerable as she was right now?

He held her as the aftershocks swept over her and then she slumped in his arms, her forehead against his shoulder as she panted against his neck. His body was screaming for release, but he couldn't have moved if he'd wanted to—and he didn't want to.

She felt so good in his arms that, for an exquisite moment, he wondered if maybe his old plan sucked and he should come up with a new one—one that involved a whole lot more Chloe and much less clothing. One where they spent the rest of the weekend in bed, learning every story their bodies had to tell.

What if…what if he'd told the truth earlier?

What if it hadn't been a lie, any of it?

"Chloe," he began, but then stopped because what the hell was he even thinking? He wasn't.

Sweet Jesus, he'd just brought Chloe Lawrence, of all people, to orgasm, which was bad enough. But he'd done it in the parking lot of a bar, out in the open where anyone could walk by and see them tangled together.

Before he'd gotten a job contract in writing.

What the *hell* was he thinking?

It only got worse when she pushed him away. He had no choice but to take that step back, no choice but to look away as she fixed her bra. "Well. That was…" She cleared her throat. "Well."

That was *bad*, that's what that was. And he had no idea what he could say that wouldn't make things worse. All of his blood had abandoned his brain for his groin, clearly. Best laid plans and all that crap.

He adjusted his pants and winced. "Yeah."

"Right." Then, without another word, she turned and walked off into the darkness.

Hell. He couldn't have screwed this up worse if he'd tried.

He better start hoping for a miracle.

Seven

By the time Chloe arrived at the rodeo the next afternoon, she was on the verge of throwing up the half cup of yogurt she'd managed to choke down that morning.

She hadn't slept. Every time she closed her eyes, Pete appeared before her, his body pressing hers against the truck, his hands everywhere.

She'd let him do that.

Let? Hell. She'd practically *ordered* him to do that.

Him. Pete Wellington. In public.

Christ.

She'd played right into his hand—literally. Short of doing a striptease for him on the bar, she'd given him everything he needed to either blackmail her for her silence or oh-so-publicly cut her to shreds and honestly, Chloe had no idea which one was worse.

Because they both led to the same place—her losing control of the All-Stars.

The only question was, how would he play his hand? Because he held all the cards. And Chloe could barely move her fingers on her right hand.

She walked around the arena, forcing herself to say hello to the people she passed. Years of smiling big while galloping around the arena paid off. But it wasn't easy because no one met her gaze or returned her greetings. What the hell? So she smiled harder, made sure to say good morning a little louder, but people's gazes still cut away from hers.

Great. Wonderful. Pete had fed her a sob story about how he'd seen the light and become a better man and then he'd gotten her into a compromising position and there would be no grace period. He'd already run his mouth and told everyone about last night. As plans went to turn *her* crew and riders against her, it was brutally efficient.

She made it to her closet and got the door shut before her face crumpled. She needed a counterattack here. So he'd gotten her off? So what? She enjoyed orgasms as much as the next girl and heavens knew it'd been too long since her last assisted one. And who could blame her for taking advantage of what Pete had offered? He was ruggedly handsome and so damn *good* with his hands.

But she would not be ashamed of her sexuality,

by God. And anyone who tried to make her feel that way would live to regret it.

Yes, she could do this. Pete had used her? Two could play at this game. She'd used *him*. She'd been in the mood and he'd been convenient. Simple as that. It was his problem if he couldn't tell the difference.

Yeah, that was a good attitude going forward but this was still going to be the most awkward day ever. To say nothing of what Flash would do when he found out. God, she hoped the police wouldn't have to get involved.

A knock on the door made her start, but not as much as Pete's voice saying, "Chloe? Are you dressed?"

She shuddered. Okay, so they were doing this now.

Taking a deep breath, she spun and threw the door open, glaring at him. "Does this meet your high standards?" she snapped, waving her hand over her favorite pair of leggings, the ones where the pattern looked like a cozy fall sweater in purples.

"Whoa," he said, throwing his hands up in surrender. Again. He did that a lot around her. "Easy."

"I am not your freaking horse, Pete, and there is nothing *easy* about this."

He rubbed at the back of his neck. "Okay, that answers one question. But," he hurried on before she could dissect that statement, "we have bigger problems."

"Bigger than you telling everyone you got me off in a parking lot?"

"For God's sake," he hissed, pushing her back

into the dressing room and kicking the door closed behind her, "keep your voice down! What is wrong with you?"

"I'm trapped in a closet with a serial liar and con man?" She retreated back against the dressing room table, which was as far as she could go. Crossing her arms over her chest, she glared at him. "Why the hell did you tell everyone about what happened last night?"

He goggled at her. "What? No—that's—where did you get the idea that I'd ever do something like that?"

"Oh, I don't know. Maybe by the way no one would even look at me this morning? I don't enjoy being treated like damaged goods, thank you very much."

The words shouldn't hurt, but they cut their way out of her throat and she had to look away before she did something stupid, like get all teary. She wasn't going to cry over this man. Not in this lifetime or the next.

Pete's features hardened. "I know you don't need me to defend you, but I swear to God, I will destroy the first person who treats you like that. For the record," he went on, almost shouting over Chloe's protests, "I didn't tell anyone anything about you and me because that was private and perfect. Jesus, Chloe—what kind of asshole do you take me for?"

Wait, what? Had he just said...*perfect*?

"Because," he continued, glaring at her, "whatever you think of me, I'm not that kind of jerk. I would never kiss and tell and I would never use sex to hurt a woman. For God's sake, Lawrence, give me a little credit."

She got the feeling that, if he had the room, he'd be pacing. How much of that was true? But he did look truly offended that she'd even suggest he'd do such a thing. "Did someone see us or something?"

"No," he ground out. "No one saw us. No one is talking about us at all."

"Okay…so, if that's not the problem, what is?" Because something had to have happened.

He stopped and gave her a look and she realized it wasn't a *something*, but a *someone* right as he said, "Flash got into it at the bar last night."

Her shoulders slumped. Of course. Because that was what Flash did. "With a local or with another rider?"

"Another rider."

Today was just full of surprises. Was it too late to go back in time? She'd like to restart this weekend completely.

She didn't have to ask what the fight had been about. It was always the same fight. Someone would suggest the only reason Flash did well in the rankings was his daddy owned the circuit or his sister ran the show. That was all it ever took for him to come up swinging and go down kicking. "Police?"

"And an ambulance."

Damn. "I don't suppose we'd be lucky enough that Flash was the one hospitalized?"

Pete shook his head.

"Who?"

"Tex McGraw."

Double damn. Not only was Tex one of the few people who could outride Flash, but he had several hundred thousand followers that could easily be mobilized to put Flash's head on a pike. He was popular, dammit.

And Flash wasn't. Of all the people her irritating baby brother could have gone after... She ground the heels of her palms against her eyes. "And that's why no one was feeling friendly toward me this morning."

"Could be." He cleared his throat. "But at least it wasn't personal. They aren't feeling too kindly toward any Lawrence right now."

If this were a nightmare, she'd love to wake up right now.

Alas, this was no nightmare. "How bad is Tex?"

Pete swallowed. "Broken jaw, broken knee."

"Knee?"

"Lawrences fight hard," Pete said with an attempt at a smile. But all he managed to do was look as sick as she felt. "He'll be out for the season. He's, uh, already contacted his lawyer."

"Usually Flash calls me." Because, in addition to running the rodeo, her other job was keeping Flash out of trouble. As if anyone could. "Why didn't he call me?"

Her phone rang. But it wasn't Flash, nor was it the Greater Sikeston Police Department. She glanced at the name, even more dread building. How much more dread could one person feel? "Oliver."

She needed to answer this. But...

"That'd be why, I figure." Pete took a step toward her. "Hon, I'm sorry."

"You didn't land Flash in the pokey," she replied.

He lifted her bruised hand and pressed another surprisingly tender kiss to her knuckles. "I'm sorry about how we parted last night. I'm sorry I gave you cause to worry this morning." A little of the tension drained from her shoulders. "I know we still haven't discussed the parameters of my job but..."

"Crisis management has to come first." Her phone buzzed again. "Look, Pete—"

But he beat her to the punch, so to speak. "Right. We have to protect the rodeo, first and foremost. And..." He swallowed. "And we probably shouldn't be involved while we're working together. More involved."

"Yeah." Sure, she'd been about to say that exact thing, but her pride still smarted a little. She covered it with a weak grin. "One of these days, we'll come to terms. But until then...help?"

"Always, babe. You deal with your family and the press. I'll deal with the rodeo. Okay?"

A small part of her wanted to argue against that because if Pete were really working to push her out, this was a gift-wrapped opportunity for him.

But what was she supposed to do here? Because, if the morning had been any indication, no one was going to talk to her for the rest of the weekend, much less follow her directions. Someone had to keep the rodeo on track and Pete had the skills and the connections. She needed Pete right now in a way that had nothing to do with how he filled out those Wranglers or how he'd made her feel last night.

So she swallowed her misgivings and gave her smile her level best. "Got it. Go, team?"

He leaned forward to brush a quick kiss against her lips and then he was gone, the ghost of his kiss still lingering there.

Well. At least things couldn't get any worse.

"Dare I ask what the hell you were thinking?" Chloe said, barely keeping her anger reined in. She was exhausted, worried, furious and still nauseous. But she didn't get the luxury of hiding under the covers until the world went away.

Flash might not have been carted off to the hospital, but he hadn't gotten away scot-free. Stripped of his Stetson and his boots, her little brother looked surprisingly young in jail-issue orange. He had two black eyes and the left side of his face was so swollen that he was almost unrecognizable. His knuckles were scraped raw and she could tell by the way he was sitting that he hurt.

Didn't matter. She wasn't going to feel bad for him. He had brought this on himself, just like he always did.

He looked up, his left eye completely bloodshot. Tex had gotten in a few good licks before he'd gone down. "You wouldn't understand," he said, his voice flat.

How had Chloe come to this place in her life, where the only man who treated her with anything that resembled respect was Pete Wellington? "No, I'm sure I wouldn't. I'm only your older sister and in charge of the rodeo, which, I'd like to point out, you've done more to destroy in a single night than Pete Wellington has done in ten years."

Flash tried to glare at her, but he winced in pain. "Now is not the time, sis."

"I beg to disagree," she said, feeling her temper slip through her fingers. "Because you do have time. Oliver and I agreed. You got yourself into this mess—you can get yourself right back out. You may have permanently ended the career of one of the best riders on the All-Stars circuit."

"And the biggest asshole," Flash muttered.

Chloe ignored that. She was not allowing a strong contender for that title to interrupt her tirade. "You may have torpedoed your own career in the process. And you undermined my position as a manager who can successfully run the rodeo. You don't have any friends left, Flash. No one wants to put up with this crap. Especially not me."

He crossed his arms and stared at the top of the table.

If she could reach through the mesh wire separating them, she would strangle him. "You wanted to prove that you got where you are without cashing in on the family name? Now's your chance, buddy. Because family is not going to bail you out. Not the rodeo family, and not me. You're going to sit in this jail cell. You got there all by yourself."

"You weren't there," Flash yelled, slamming his

hands down on the table. "You didn't hear the things he said. I'm not going to let any man talk about a woman the way he talked about *her*!"

Chloe had grown up with Flash. Hotheaded, short fuse, quick on the trigger—he'd always been like this. Calm and sullen one moment, raging the next. She wasn't even a little surprised about his outburst. "Her who? And what was he saying?" she asked, trying to stay calm.

If Tex had gotten sloshed and was talking about women as disrespectfully as the way those two drunks outside of Mike's had treated her, then she could at least understand why her brother had flipped out. Flash *loved* women. Sometimes too much.

If what Tex said had been abusive or even just misogynistic, Chloe needed to know before she attempted to make amends with him. She wasn't going to make someone who denigrated women the focus of any future All-Stars marketing campaigns.

Flash fell silent again. Chloe rolled her eyes. "Fine. Oliver is sending a lawyer, but you're on your own for bail and damages. You are hereby suspended from the All-Stars until further notice."

"What?" Flash exploded again, but Chloe was already standing. "You can't do this to me!"

She shook her head as she walked away. "Flash, you did this to yourself."

She was done. As she waited for the officer to open the door, she tried hard to find a silver lining in this situation. The only one she could come up with was that at least no one had caught her and Pete together.

"Does Oliver know about the deal you made with Wellington?" Flash called out behind her.

Chloe froze. Point of fact, Oliver did not. Mostly because it wasn't relevant to the current situation she was dealing with. But also because she'd put good money on the fact that Flash had already threatened Pete and she'd be willing to bet Oliver would do the same thing. Except Flash's threats tended to involve fights and Oliver's threats tended to involve expensive lawsuits.

She couldn't bring herself to lie, because lies were easy to prove wrong. But this was Flash, after all. She had no problem hedging the truth a little. "Like he cares," she said, doing her best to sneer dismissively. "The only thing Oliver cares about is that the All-Stars runs smoothly and profitably without him having to get his hands dirty. So if you think you can redirect Oliver's anger away from you and onto Wellington, I'd think twice before waving that red flag in front of that bull. Wellington isn't the reason Oliver called me this morning."

Behind her, the door clicked open and, without waiting for a reply, she turned and walked away.

She didn't even wince as the door slammed shut behind her and locked with the dull, metallic *clunk*.

Of course things got worse. Because the rodeo was family and some family squabbles could be kept quiet but this? This was not one of them. Not with the front-page headline of the *Sikeston Standard-Democrat* blaring about the fight in huge type and the editorial asking if it was safe for the town to continue hosting the rodeo.

What Chloe pieced together made it clear that the *her* in question had been Brooke Bonner, country singer and Flash's current infatuation.

As best Chloe could tell, Tex had been remarking that he didn't like Bonner because…well, the *because* was fuzzy. Tex wouldn't say much beyond Flash was a crazy bastard who was going to pay and Flash refused to say anything else in his defense. She got seven conflicting stories from eyewitnesses that ranged from Tex saying Brooke was getting fat to stating she was a no-talent hack to observing he'd "tap that," as one rider put it.

In other words, Chloe was on the losing end of the world's worst game of telephone and it was a hell of a mess. She'd say things couldn't get worse, but she wasn't about to tempt fate right now.

The All-Stars had lost Tex McGraw, most likely permanently. At the very least, he was out for the rest of the season and no force on this earth could stop him from taking swipes at Flash on social media. At least half of which Flash deserved, as far as Chloe was concerned. But worse, Tex was making plenty of noise about how he'd never ride for the All-Stars again as long as a Lawrence was in charge and maybe he'd take his skills where they'd be appreciated in the Total Bull Challenge.

Flash was booked for assault and sued accordingly and Chloe refused to overturn his indefinite suspension, which meant two of the All-Stars' top ten riders were out. No one wanted Flash back, that much was clear. His hot temper had caught fire too many times and all his bridges had burned to ash.

Chloe looked weak as a leader because she couldn't manage her brother or the bad press. Even announcing that Flash had been suspended, pending trial dates, didn't help much. Somehow, she was responsible for Flash's behavior, which infuriated her all over again. Flash was a twenty-four-year-old adult. He was responsible for his own screw-ups. Not her. She wasn't her brother's keeper, dammit.

And what had she been doing when this whole thing had gone down? Getting to third base with Pete.

Chloe was comfortable with her decision to leave Flash locked up, but that didn't mean she still didn't have to clean up after his messes. Everywhere the rodeo landed, it felt like she gave the exact same interview. Yes, the All-Stars were hopeful that Tex McGraw would make a full and complete recovery. Yes, the All-Stars were doing everything they could to assist Tex in achieving that goal. Yes, Flash was suspended pending his trial for assault. No, Chloe had not personally been there when the fight broke out. No, she didn't know what had started it all. No, she hadn't heard any rumors swirling that somehow linked the brawl back to Brooke Bonner.

She'd love to talk about the changes coming to the All-Stars—but no one wanted to ask about those.

They all wanted to prop up the click-bait headlines that seemed to follow the Lawrence family no matter where they went. Unfortunately, Flash's trouble with the law was the perfect opportunity to resurface all those terrible facts about the Preston Pyramid scheme and how the former Renee Preston, current Renee Lawrence, was related to the very criminals who'd ruined everyone's life.

There might not be such a thing as bad PR, but Chloe could do with a lot less of it.

The good news—because she was still clinging to whatever silver lining she could—was that not only did Pete Wellington do a damned fine job running the All-Stars while Chloe handled the media and the lawyers and, worst of all, her family, but he announced the changes she'd told him about when they had been sitting in the back of a pickup truck what felt like years ago.

Next season, women would be allowed to compete in both the team events and the individual events. Yes, it was infuriating that, for the most part, everyone nodded and smiled and said something along the lines of, *well, maybe it was about time*. Chloe knew damned well that if she'd announced the changes, she would've gotten nothing but heartbreak and heartburn. But those same ideas coming out of Wellington's mouth? Everyone signed on with remarkably little dissent.

Which was good for the rodeo. Not so much for her ego.

She rarely got the chance to talk to Pete, and when

she did, they kept the conversations short and focused on the tasks at hand. He kept her up-to-date on what the riders were talking about and she apprised him of the media chatter. He didn't barge in to her dressing room anymore and she didn't ask him to get something to eat. They were both too busy keeping the All-Stars from collapsing under its own weight. And besides, they'd agreed—they couldn't be anything more than coworkers. It was better this way.

Except…except when she mounted up and waited to make her entrance into the arena, she looked for him. And she usually found him, on top of one of the chutes, watching her with what felt like far more than friendly interest. Every single time their gazes met, heat flashed down her back and she wished he'd barge into her dressing room, just one more time.

For those few moments, separated by fences and horses and cowboys, she wasn't the Lawrence in charge and he wasn't the de facto rodeo manager. When her gaze met his and he gave her that wink, she could still feel his hands on her body, still taste him on her tongue. And given the way he stared at her, she couldn't help but wonder if he felt the same.

But she wasn't going to ask. Yeah, for that brief moment in time against the side of his truck, she'd just been Chloe and he'd been Pete and there hadn't been any past betrayals or family dramas. They'd only been a man and a woman outside a honky-tonk bar on a Friday night and it'd been *good*.

Too bad she might never get another moment like that.

Eight

The woman's voice cut through the hotel lobby. "What do you mean, I don't have a reservation?"

Chloe?

Pete's head whipped up so fast that he almost tripped over his own boots. Desire slammed into his gut. It *was* Chloe. There was no mistaking that backside in those stretch pants. She normally got to the rodeo a day before he did, but the way the flights to Pendleton, Oregon, had worked out, he was here early.

Good thing, too. As he got closer, he could see she was physically shaking.

The clerk behind the desk looked mortified as he apologized profusely, saying, "I'm so sorry but there's no record of a reservation under that name and we're booked solid—there's a convention in town and then the rodeo. There isn't a room in town." He cleared his throat, looking as hopeful as possible. "Did someone else make the reservation?"

"No, I did. I thought…" Her voice broke as she dropped her head onto her forearms.

The clerk shot Pete a pleading look, one that begged for patience.

This should have been Pete's moment of victory and he hadn't even done anything to earn it. Chloe was about to crack under the pressure of running the rodeo, just like he'd known she would. She was going to fall apart and Pete would be right here to pick up the pieces and show the world that Chloe Lawrence didn't have what it took—while he did.

Except… Her back rose and fell with a shuddering breath.

This wasn't right. He wanted her out of the All-Stars, but did he really want her broken?

Dammit all, he didn't.

"Problem?" he asked.

Chloe spun around. She looked terrible—pale, with dark circles under her eyes and so obviously upset. What the hell? His Chloe wouldn't buckle just because of a wayward reservation.

He moved without thinking, dropping his bag and pulling her into his arms. "What's wrong, hon?"

She took a ragged breath as her arms wrapped around his waist and she all but crumpled into him. Chloe Lawrence *clung* to him as if he were a rock in the middle of the stormy sea. "I don't have a room and there are no rooms and it's been a terrible week and…" She took another shuddering breath and Pete knew she was trying not to cry.

He hugged her harder, his heart pounding. He had seen Chloe angry, defensive, seductive, flirty and happy. She always looked so danged happy sitting at the head of the procession in her princess finery, ready to ride and wearing the hell out of her chaps.

He'd wanted her back in his arms, wanted her vulnerable and open like she'd been against the side of his truck. But this? He didn't want her destroyed. The urge to fix this mess was almost overwhelming.

He wanted to help her.

The realization left him feeling dazed. The burr under his saddle that was Chloe Lawrence? The thorn in his backside that he'd give anything to be rid of? He was being gifted with a golden opportunity to finish the job he'd started.

Her body was pressed against his and he realized he was stroking her hair. He couldn't do it, dammit. Fool that he was, he was going to protect her. Didn't matter from what. What mattered was that she needed someone on her side right now and by God, Pete was going to be that man.

She stiffened in his arms and pulled away, blinking hard. "Sorry, sorry," she said, trying to smile— or maybe look confident and in control? Either way, she failed miserably. "Just a little tired."

He leaned down, his mouth close to her ear. "You're a terrible liar." Her cheeks shot red as he added in a regular voice, "I have a room and you're taking it. I'll find another hotel."

"You can't do that," she said, like she had a choice in the matter. "There aren't any rooms!"

He stepped around her. "Wellington, Peter. I should have a reservation?" Looking relieved, the clerk nodded and started tapping on the keys.

Pete could hear Chloe huffing behind him. He grinned. Giving his room to Chloe was the right thing to do. Besides, it would go a long way toward earning her trust. He'd kept his nose clean for the last month, doing nothing that would make her suspicious of his ulterior motives.

Of course, he hadn't exactly had the time to work on any of those ulterior motives. Flash Lawrence had screwed up his plans but good. Just keeping the wheels from falling off the All-Stars took everything he had and that was with Chloe managing the marketing and PR and high-level decisions. He should be grateful for the chance to start pushing her out.

Why wasn't he?

He cut a glance to her. She was somewhere between confused and…angry, maybe? "Pete, what are you doing?" she asked. At least she didn't sound shattered anymore.

"If it's not obvious, then I'm doing it wrong," he replied with a wink. That got him a full-on glare which, oddly, made Pete felt better. If he were going to best Chloe Lawrence, he wanted her to go down fighting. There was no pride in kicking her when she was already down.

"Sir?" the clerk said. "We have you down for a king suite, no smoking. How many keys?"

Pete looked back at Chloe. She'd gotten close enough to touch and oh, how he wanted to touch her. What would it be like if this wasn't an accident? What if they'd planned to get in a night early and spend the evening wrapped up in each other? He had to shift his legs to relieve the pressure. "One," he said, nodding in her direction. "Give it to her."

"No, wait." She touched him on the upper arm, her lower lip tucked under her teeth. "You can't drive off tonight. It isn't right."

He snorted. "I'm not the kind of man who would kick a woman to the curb when there's a perfectly fine room available."

Her hand flattened on his arm, sending heat through the fabric of his shirt. Last time she'd touched him, there'd been too many clothes and not enough bare skin. "Pete…" she said, his name soft on her lips. "Maybe we could share?" She said it like she knew it was a bad idea.

And it was. It was a freaking terrible idea because he didn't want to be a gentleman about Chloe and a king-size bed. He turned into her to warn her off but the movement brought their bodies close together and that night against his pickup truck, where he'd made her come apart under his touch—it all came roaring back to him.

He could do a lot more than make her shatter in a hurried series of blunt touches dulled through layers of fabric. He could strip her down slowly, properly worshipping each inch of skin he revealed like the goddess she was.

He shook his head, trying to get a grip, but it wasn't easy. She was only inches away, staring up at him with her big brown eyes. What would a gentleman do? Hell if he could remember because he did not want to be a gentleman right now. He wanted to give and take and give some more until Chloe was breathless beneath him, his name a cry of pleasure on her lips.

He shifted again. It didn't do a damned thing for the roaring erection barely being held in check by his belt buckle. "Are you sure that's a good idea?"

Her eyes darkened and he saw her throat work to swallow. No, it wasn't a good idea. But she said, "It'll be fine, I'm sure."

Oh, he was sure, too. Sure he could bare her body and be inside of her in minutes, if not sooner. He wanted her naked this time, her body spread open for him to feast on.

The gentlemanly thing to do would be pick up his bag, do an about-face and march his butt right back out to his car. If he drove long enough, he'd find a small town with a room available. The smart thing to do would be to put as much distance between him and this woman as possible.

Pete had never claimed to be *that* smart.

The clerk cleared his throat. "How many keys?"

Pete cupped her cheek in his hand, watching her eyelashes flutter at the touch. She was so warm, so soft. "You can have the room."

It wasn't his last grasp at decency, but it was damned close.

Chloe took a long breath and said, "Two, please. But I'm paying you back for the room, Wellington."

He chuckled. Yeah, this was how he wanted her—a battle of the equals. God, he liked her like this. "Like hell you are, Lawrence." He turned to the clerk. "Two keys. One bill."

The clerk nodded, his relief obvious. He made promises about giving Chloe extra rewards points and maybe Pete got some, too—he wasn't paying attention. He was busy trying to game plan the rest of his night.

The mess Flash had made had been both a blessing and a curse. It had kept Pete busy trying to reassure everyone associated with each All-Stars rodeo—riders and contractors, not to mention the local rodeo boards—that the All-Stars was safe and solid and going strong. The other parts of his plan had languished under the sheer amount of work he had to do, but he was happy to do it because he wanted his rodeo back in one piece, not in tattered remains.

But it was a blessing, too, because even though he hadn't moved forward with his plans to push Chloe out, it'd happened almost by accident anyway. She dealt with the press, smoothing over the losses of both Tex and Flash. She handled the marketing and distribution and her clothing line. She hadn't dealt with a single stock contractor in almost a month.

How much would it take to turn the contractors away from her?

The clerk handed her both keys and she turned to him. "Shall we?"

"Let's."

That one blisteringly hot moment against his truck notwithstanding, Chloe was making it almost too easy to wall her off from the day-to-day operations. As long as Pete could keep his hands and other body parts to himself, he could just keep on letting things play out. The further Chloe got from the running of the actual rodeo, the harder it would be for her to step back in and the more people would resist Pete leaving.

On the other hand, he had one night alone in a hotel room with her. This was the sort of opportunity that didn't come around every day. But was it worth it, wrapping himself up further in her?

They walked down the hall to the elevator silently. Chloe clutched both key cards in her hand. All Pete needed to do was to keep walking out the other exit door at the end of this hall and back out to the parking lot. That was it.

But then she turned to him as the elevator door dinged open and said, "Coming?"

To hell with his long-term plans. Chloe was a once-in-a-lifetime opportunity and he'd be a fool to pass her up. "Yeah."

They maneuvered their bags into the elevator and stood silently as the door closed. Pete gave her to the count of three to lay down her rules, but all she did was fiddle with the key cards. So he took the reins. "Thinking about how you want this to go?"

She startled and stared at him with her huge eyes. "What?"

"Tonight. How you want this to go." She blinked a few times at him, her mouth opened slightly. Was he imagining things or was she breathing harder? "The way I see it, we have three options."

No, he wasn't imagining it. Her body canted toward his ever so slightly. "And those are?"

He was more than tempted to press her against the back of the elevator and skip the first two options. But this was his very last attempt at decency. "The first option is that I spend the night on the sofa while you sleep on the far side of the king bed and neither of us moves for fear of disturbing the other, leaving us tired and cranky tomorrow."

Her brow wrinkled. "That's an option?"

"Not my favorite. Or," he went on, "option two is that we decide we're rational, mature adults who can share a bed while keeping our hands to ourselves and then, in a bold display of that maturity, we line up pillows down the center of the bed so we each stay on our own side. We'll lay awake all night, staring at the ceiling, wondering if the other person is thinking the same thing we are, leaving us tired, cranky *and* frustrated tomorrow."

The elevator began to slow as they reached their floor. "So, that leaves option three as…"

He reached out, stroking his fingertips over the curve of her cheek. "We take a small break from our previous agreement that, as coworkers, we shouldn't spend the night together and then whatever happens, happens."

A furrow appeared between her eyebrows but even so, she leaned into his touch. Not a lot, but enough. "*Whatever*, huh?"

He grinned. Because that had not been a *no*.

"Let me love on you a little, Chloe. I'll take care of you tonight. Tomorrow, we can go back to the way we were."

"What if we can't?"

It was a fair question and one he didn't have an answer to. He stroked her skin as the elevator doors opened. With a nod of his head toward the hallway before them, he replied, "Then we go forward as best we can."

She gasped as he grabbed her bag and headed toward the room. After a moment, he heard her behind him.

He had to stop at the door and wait for her because she held all the cards here—key and otherwise. She didn't look at him as she unlocked the door, but she held it open for him, so that counted for something. He set her bag down on the bed but left his on the floor. Then he crossed to the small desk and flipped on the light.

When he turned around, Chloe was half in shadows. Every fiber of his being was screaming to go to her, to pull her into his arms and kiss her hard, to make that decision for her. Or at least, make it easier. But he didn't want to overwhelm her better angels because he knew if he did, tomorrow would be that much harder. Worse, because tomorrow they wouldn't have Flash's messes to clean up. It would, God willing, be a normal day at a normal rodeo.

Speaking of… "What about the rodeo?" she asked, taking a small step toward the light.

"What about it?"

She gave him a dull look. "Look, option three is a bad idea twice over. Either you'll hold *whatever* over my head in this plot you're working on to steal the rodeo away or we'll still be coworkers who shouldn't even attempt the maturity of pillow barriers."

Yeah, that stung. He hadn't said a damned thing about what'd happened in Missouri, except to tell her he wouldn't use sex against her. But then again, he couldn't blame her for being cautious. "Either you trust me or you don't."

She looked away first, running her hands through her hair. "I'm going to take a shower. I had a bad meeting and a terrible flight and—" she swallowed. "And I'm grateful that you're sharing the room with me."

Hell. He crossed the room in a few long strides and pulled her into his arms. "I'm sorry you had a crappy day," he said into her hair.

She stiffened, as if she expected him to press his case, but all he did was hold her and after a long moment, she melted into him. "It did suck," she admitted. "What are you doing here early?"

He chuckled. "Do you know how hard it is to get from East Texas to this part of Oregon? It would've been less painful if I'd driven. What was your meeting?"

"Oh, that." She sighed heavily, causing her chest to rub against his. "Family stuff."

That couldn't be good. If Milt or Oliver Lawrence decided to take a more active role in the All-Stars, Pete would be in danger of losing everything he'd worked for because he wasn't exactly on friendly terms with either man.

But then again, this was the Lawrence family, so he made an educated guess. "Flash causing trouble again?"

She didn't quite pull off a grin, but the eye roll was classic Chloe. "You have no idea."

"No," he murmured, lowering his head to hers, "but I'm starting to get one."

Unlike the kiss a month ago, this was not hard or hurried. It was a soft meeting of the lips, a promise of something more. Chloe's arms tightened around his waist, making her breasts press against his chest and his groin hit her hipbone. Fire licked through his veins and he started praying that she'd decided on option three because *frustrated* was not going to be strong enough to describe his state if he had to bunk down on the sofa.

Her tongue traced the seam of his lips and he almost groaned at the touch because it sure seemed like option three was going to be the big winner. But instead he pulled away and forced himself to say, "You—shower."

Which was not the most verbose thing he'd ever

said, but it was all he was capable of. Another moment in her arms, and he wouldn't be able to walk away. Hell, he wouldn't be able to walk, not with the erection he was working on.

She nodded and took that all-important step away, touching her fingertips to her lips as if she couldn't believe he had just kissed her.

When she got to the bathroom door, she looked back. The full force of her desire hit him hard and threatened to send him to his knees. But before he could take another step toward her, she closed the door and shot the lock.

Oh, yeah. It was stupid to risk everything for a night with Chloe, but one thing was clear—that woman was worth it.

Nine

What the hell was she doing?

That was the question Chloe asked herself repeatedly as hot water sluiced over her shoulders and down her back. The fact that she was even considering spending the night with Pete was insane. What happened before in Missouri had been…just one of those things. Her adrenaline had been pumping from the fight and she'd needed to let off a little steam. She hadn't been there for Pete—he'd just been the safest, most convenient option. They'd gotten swept up in the moment and that was that. No big deal.

And this was Pete Wellington, for heaven's sake. The man had done his level best to make her life a living hell for the last ten and a half years. At every turn, he had criticized, undermined and generally made a huge pain of himself. She could still hear her father's ranting in her ear from this morning, demanding to know how she could dare trust him, how she could dare risk the All-Stars? Or, worse, when Dad had stopped yelling long enough to take a breath, Oliver's sullen glares and his quiet accusation, "I thought you said you could handle the rodeo yourself."

Yeah, well—that had been before Flash had committed assault *and* before Flash made good on his promise to tell Dad and Oliver about Pete unless Chloe ended his suspension early so he could ride again.

It'd also been before Pete had turned out not to be the villain she had pegged him for.

The next time she saw Flash, she was going to wring his neck. The nerve of that idiot. Seriously, all he did was get pissed whenever someone suggested he'd only gotten ranked in the All-Stars because he traded on the family name. But the moment things got messy, what did Flash do? Tried to blackmail his own sister so he could get around the rules that applied to everyone else.

By God, if he had the nerve to show up at the rodeo in two days' time and do anything that even looked like *smirk*, she was going to finish him, and he'd deserve it.

She heard a thump from the room. Flash was *a* problem but he wasn't *the* problem she had to deal with right now. That honor went to Pete freaking

Wellington and his thoughtful gift of a hotel room and his tempting offers to take care of her.

She shouldn't even be considering option three. She should offer to take the sofa or sleep on the floor or anything, really, that kept at least a modicum of distance between her and Pete.

But she was considering it. Oh, she was.

If it were just because he'd brought her to a shattering orgasm in less than five minutes with nothing more than his fingers, that'd be enough of a reason to give him a second chance. He'd been hot stuff back when she'd first laid eyes on him almost ten years ago, and since then? Pete was the finest of wines, getting better with age until he was perfect. And last time, she hadn't gotten to see the rest of him. She'd barely gotten to touch him.

She wanted him. Not just for a quick climax—although she was never one to pass on those. A night with him loving on her? God, she'd never heard anything so tempting as that.

And then he had to go and offer up his room—multiple times—before he'd even mentioned option three. She had no doubt he could take care of her sexual needs but the man had made her health and well-being his priority and *that* was a dangerous thing. She knew how to protect herself from the Pete Wellington who hated her guts, detested her brothers and lived to exact his revenge on her father.

She didn't know how to protect herself from the Pete who cared for her.

Ever since he'd barged into her dressing room a

month ago, he'd done nothing but defend her, promote her ideas and who could forget about the orgasm? For the last month, he'd worked his butt off for the All-Stars and there hadn't been so much as a single whisper of betrayal.

She wasn't so stupid that she hadn't been checking up on him. Of course she had. He was doing his job well. Sadly, better than she could because no one wanted to take the All-Stars in a new direction simply because the Princess of the Rodeo said so.

But all of her ideas, coming from Pete? People got on board. Fast.

Truly, it had been an awful day. And there was no guarantee that her father or Oliver or, worst of all, Flash wouldn't show up at this weekend's rodeo and cause all sorts of trouble. No, the worst would be if all three of them came together.

She shuddered and pushed the thought from her mind. The important thing was that they weren't here now—Pete was, with his thoughtful gestures and full-on charm, his good hugs and better kisses, his beautiful damned eyes and hot body.

And his bed. His big, soft bed.

She ran her hands over her breasts. They were heavy and tight and she knew what'd make them feel better. Some things had changed in a month and one of those things—the only relevant one at the moment, it seemed—was the fact that she wanted him again. *Still*. A month of pretending she had no interest in Pete was just that—pretending.

Better, he still wanted her. A man didn't casually

mention sex if he weren't ready, willing and able to deliver the goods.

A knock on the bathroom door startled her so hard that she almost slipped. "Yes?"

"Got to get something. I'll be back in a bit."

"Oh. Okay." She heard the room door open and then realized—he might be leaving. "Pete?" she yelled in a panic because if he decided to be all noble, she'd kill him for leaving her aching for his touch.

"Yeah?" his voice came right back to the bath-room door.

"You're coming back, right?"

There was a pause that was long. Too long. Damn that man, he was torturing her, wasn't he? He'd brought up the possibility of sex and thrown in that gentle kiss and now he was going to leave her high and dry and—

"Do you want me to?" Even through the door and over the sound of the shower running, his voice reso-nated through her body.

Everything about her tightened and she came piti-fully close to climbing out of the shower and drag-ging him onto the bed. "Yes." She swallowed, her hand gripping the shower curtain. "Please."

"Then I'll see you in a few."

As lines went, it wasn't the most romantic thing she'd ever heard. But there was no denying the relief that coursed through her as the door shut. Hopefully, he'd remembered to grab a key.

He was coming back. For her.

She wanted him. It was that simple. She wanted

him, and she could have him. Was that a problem? After all, they'd been able to do this before—engage in certain liberties and then go on as if nothing had happened. What's to say they couldn't do that again?

Just for one night. They'd overlook the sound business practice of keeping business and personal separate and whatever happened…happened.

If she were really lucky, *whatever* would happen several times. But only this once and then things would go back to the way they'd been before.

She dropped her head into her hands. This wasn't the sort of thing that people could pretend had never happened. This would change everything between her and Pete. And yet, she was going to let that man love on her and hold her all night long because…

No. She didn't need him. Absolutely not. But she needed *something* and he was here.

Oh, she was in trouble, wasn't she?

Her mind made up, she took her time shaving her legs and moisturizing. Because it made her feel better, not because she was primping for a man. Or even one specific man.

She was in the middle of brushing her teeth when the door clicked open and Pete said, "It's me."

A thrill shot through her. He'd kept his word. "I'm almost done."

"Honey," he said through the door, his voice warm and rich, "I'd wait all night for you."

Her breasts tightened almost to the point of pain and heat flooded her center. "Would you really?"

"Yup. But, Chloe?"

She forced herself to breath. The woman looking back at her in the steamy mirror was nude and aroused and cupping her own breasts. But it wasn't enough. She needed more. "Yes?" It came out needy.

He could tell—she heard it in his voice when he said, "Don't make me wait forever."

She was absolutely not going to open this door and throw herself at him. Nope. She might desperately want everything he was offering, but she wasn't about to come off as desperate. A girl still had her pride.

He could just keep waiting, even if only for another five minutes. She forced herself to go slow as she slid her nightgown over her head. It wasn't a peek-a-boo lace teddy or anything. She liked to sleep in a dove gray silk slip that came to almost her knees. But when she looked in the mirror, she could see the hard points of her nipples and, really, what more did a girl need when it came to seduction?

She twisted her damp hair into a messy high bun so it would dry with curls in it and then, taking a deep breath, she walked out into the room.

And stumbled to a stop at the sight of Pete in a white T-shirt, his buckle undone and the top two buttons on his fly hanging open. He wasn't naked, not even close. But dear God, he was a wonder to behold. Had she ever properly appreciated his biceps? Or his forearms? The muscles bulged as he worked a cork loose from a bottle of wine. Her gaze dropped to those open buttons and the faint outline of a bulge still hidden that promised amazing things.

He popped the cork and looked up. His jaw fell open and he almost dropped the bottle. The cork was a lost cause. "My God, Chloe," he murmured with what sounded like awe. "Look at you."

She wouldn't have thought it possible, but her nipples got even harder. She positively ached for his touch. But again, she didn't fling herself at him. Instead, she skimmed her hands over the cool silk of her nightie. His eyes almost bulged out of his head.

This was good. She'd had a hot shower and time to calm down and she wasn't some delicate flower. She was his equal, by God, and she was going to make him sweat. Was he even breathing? When he lifted his gaze to her face, he seemed dazed. She nodded toward the bottle—*not* his bulge, which looked like it was actively growing. "Is that for me?"

He seemed startled to realize he was holding an open bottle. "Oh. The wine. Yes, and some chocolate," he added. "And ice cream. Vanilla's okay?"

Sweet merciful heavens, this man. She couldn't remember the last time a man had brought her chocolate, much less wine and ice cream. How was she supposed to be all cool and seductive when she was so stupidly grateful he was here?

Chloe had put a hand over her chest to try to keep her heart from beating so hard he'd be able to see it.

"Where did you get all of this?"

He stood, grinning. She felt a little dazed, too. "I have my ways." He grabbed another glass from next to another ice bucket—which was full of ice—and poured her some white wine.

"I can't remember the last time I had someone do something this nice for me." She wasn't including Renee in that, though. Girlfriends operated at a different level than men she was sleeping with. And right now, Pete was blowing every other man she'd ever known out of the water.

He handed her the glass of wine. When Chloe took it, she let her fingers skim over his. His breath caught in his throat, but he held her gaze and said, "That's a damned shame. You deserve nice things, Chloe."

She looked up at him. "What if…" She swallowed. They'd already had almost-sex. He'd already offered even more sex. Why did she suddenly feel so shy? "What if I want more than *nice*?"

He was suddenly in front of her, the heat radiating off his chest, warming her through her silk slip. She tensed when he lifted a hand but instead of pulling her into his arms, he wrapped one curl around his finger. He whispered, "You deserve every good thing, babe," then he kissed that little curl, his chest coming flush with hers. "And I want to give it to you. Anything you want, it's yours."

This time, she did melt into him, as best she could while holding a glass of wine. Her arm went around his waist, bringing her chest flush with his and, as her nipples slid against the warming silk, they went rock-hard.

Pete released her wayward curl and brushed his lips over her ear. "Did you decide?" His breath caressed her skin and then his teeth tugged on her earlobe.

"Did you really get me wine and chocolate?" It was a stupid question because of course he had. Those things hadn't materialized out of thin air. But he'd gone out of his way and done something wonderfully sweet. For her.

He was the most dangerous man she'd ever known.

"Darlin'," he said, his voice pure Texas drawl as his lips skimmed over her jaw, "I'm starting to think that there's not much I wouldn't do for you."

Oh. *Oh, my.* "Option three," she breathed. "Please."

She didn't know if she kissed him or if he kissed her or if it even mattered. Pete was here, for her.

"Just for the night," she murmured as he took the glass of wine from her hands and pivoted to set it on the table, turning her at the same time. Her back hit the wall and then he was pressing against her.

"Well," he chuckled, running one hand down her thigh and lifting her leg so it wrapped around his waist, "maybe the morning, too."

She gasped as his erection bumped against her sex. "God, yes," she managed to get out, but then Pete was kissing her, devouring her and she gave herself over to him.

What she needed was this man, hot and hard against her. He nipped at her lower lip as his hips rocked into her and she couldn't fight back the moan.

"Could I make you come, just like this?" he growled against the skin of her neck, thrusting against her. He had one hand holding up her leg, the other braced against the wall by her head. Her arms around his neck, she hung on for the ride.

Chloe whimpered. It wasn't dignified or logical, but this man had the ability to reduce her to panting desperation in a matter of seconds. Standing up, even! And not for the first time. How good would he be in an actual bed?

He rocked against her and she bit down on his neck, which made him groan. "I think you're going to come for me," he said, but his voice was rough and she knew he felt it, too—this connection between them, however tenuous it was. "Then I'm going to lay you out on that bed and make love to you until you come again."

She shuddered at the words, the tension coiling inside her becoming sharper, almost painful. How did he do this to her?

But he did. Easily. The hand under her leg pushed the hem of the slip up. Not that the silk was a great barrier between their bodies but when he lifted it out of the way, she gasped as she came into contact with the stiff denim of his jeans.

"So beautiful," he got out in a strained whisper, his forehead resting on hers. Her eyes flew open and what she saw reflected in his gaze made her gasp again.

Please let this be real. She didn't think that on purpose, but there it was. She wanted *whatever* this was with Pete to be real.

That feeling only got stronger when he repeated, "God, Chloe. So damned beautiful." But this time, he pulled his other hand away from the wall and covered her breast with it, pulling the silk tight over her nipple. Then he kissed her as he squeezed.

And Chloe came for him, moaning loudly as the tension in her body snapped back. He sucked down the noise and didn't stop thrusting against her, not even when her legs began to shake. Everything began to shake, and she knew she was in danger of falling. She pulled away from his mouth and said, "I can't stand."

And that man had the damned nerve to wink at her. And pivot his hips so his erection ground against her. "That," he said, sounding way too pleased with himself, "was the plan."

She liked a confident partner, she really did. But this was beyond confident. This was Pete like she knew him—cocky. Convinced he knew best. And okay, maybe he did. But he wasn't in charge here.

She was. And it was high time he remembered that.

She pushed at his chest, but that barely moved him, so she used the wall for leverage. "You forgot something," she said, managing to keep her balance as he stumbled back and dropped her leg.

"What?" But he didn't look worried or even mildly concerned. Instead, he had that teasing smile tucked into the corners of his lips.

She took a deep breath, making sure her knees were going to hold before she stepped toward him. "You work *underneath* me."

The man licked his lips and then Chloe was pulling his shirt over his head and shoving his jeans and shorts down. Then she pushed him, and he fell back onto the bed with a muffled *whump*. And he grinned at her the whole time, like he'd just found the golden ticket.

She stared at his body, hoping her mouth was shut. Good lord, the man was built. His chest was broad and muscled without being fastidiously ripped. A working man's muscles, ones he'd earned the hard way. But that wasn't the part that caught her attention. Oh, no. She couldn't look away from his erection, hard and long and curved ever-so-slightly to the right. He was big without being huge and he hadn't manscaped. She liked that hair on him, liked the calluses on his hands. She liked him rough around the edges but most of all, she liked him underneath her.

As she looked her fill, he twisted until he was able to reach his back pocket, where he grabbed a small box of condoms. "Yes?" he asked, tossing them on the bed.

She shot him a look. "You were counting on option three, weren't you?"

He didn't even have the decency to blush. "Been waiting for this moment for a month, hon." He kicked the rest of the way out of his jeans and propped himself up on his elbows, his legs draped over the edge of the bed. "Ever since Missouri, I haven't been able to get you off my mind, so you're damned right I'd want to be prepared. I want to see you this time."

She mounted up and straddled him, smacking his hands away when he tried to lift her slip over her head. "Hey," he protested but then she settled on him, his thick erection rubbing against her sex.

"I'm the boss," she told him when he reached for the slip again. This time, she grabbed his hands and held them tight, using his arms to help her stay balanced. Instead of fighting her, he laced his fingers with hers and another part of her melted. She was still shaky, her pulse still pounding through her sex as the last of the climax worked through her. Without layers of fabric between them, she could feel the heat of his body against hers, the pulse of his erection as she slid back and forth. "Pete," she started but then stopped because she wasn't sure what she was going to say next.

As she moved over him, his head fell back and he began to pant. "You're killing me, Lawrence," he moaned, his body quaking under hers.

"Just returning the favor." But even as she said it, that tension began to coil within her body again. For a month, they'd both been dreaming of this moment. Every time she caught him watching her from the top of the chutes, this was the heat that flashed down her body. All roads led here. It'd been pointless to fight it, she realized. This time was theirs.

This time, she wanted him inside her.

So she scooted back and reached for the condoms. Now it was Pete who batted her hands away and got the packet open. "I could have done that," she scolded as he quickly rolled the condom on.

"And let you keep torturing me?" He tried to give

her another cocky grin, but that was when Chloe peeled the slip off.

And held her breath. Pete sucked in air as he stared. She arched her back to put her perfectly average breasts in the best light. After her second boyfriend had taken one look at her bare breasts and said in a pitying tone, "they're not *that* bad," she'd made a concerted effort to master all the tricks to make them look their best. Arch the back, suck in the stomach, try not to lie flat on her back lest her poor breasts all but disappear.

So she braced herself because she was naked in bed with Pete Wellington and he could be the man of her dreams and he could still also cut her to shreds if he wanted to.

Did he want to?

He sat up and stroked his fingers over the tops of her breasts, over her nipples. Then he leaned forward and pressed his lips to the tip of her left breast. "Perfect," he murmured against her skin and then he sucked her whole nipple into his mouth.

"Oh, God," she whispered, clutching his head as his teeth skimmed over her delicate skin. The pull of his mouth drew an answering pull from deep inside her. His sheathed erection continued to rub against her from below and it was just that damned easy for him to take her breath away.

There was no negotiation about how it was his turn, how he needed to let go, how he couldn't wait another second. He didn't push or rush or demand.

Instead, he just sucked at her sensitive skin and let her body bear down on his as he took his sweet time.

This was what it meant to let a man love on her. To let a man take care of her. She'd had plenty of boyfriends and lovers but she'd never had a man who put her first like this. For heaven's sake, she was already naked and he had on the condom!

But instead of lifting her bottom and thrusting into her, he just kissed his way to her other breast and began to torment that nipple, too.

She stared down at him as he lavished her with attention, her fingers twined in his thick hair. It almost didn't feel real, this moment with him. But if it was a dream, she didn't want to wake up.

Finally, she couldn't take it anymore. She needed him inside of her. "Lie back." She didn't have to tell him twice.

Chloe scooted forward, raising her bottom in the air as she kissed him. His erection sprang up against her and, because she was absolutely not done torturing him, she let herself sink back onto him—slowly. Years of gripping a saddle with her thighs while she rode around arenas gave her the strength to move so slowly that Pete began to cuss.

"Dammit, Chloe," he growled, trying to sit up and thrust into her.

She shoved him by his shoulders until he was flat on his back and shifted until she had his thighs pinned to the bed with her feet. "My turn, Pete. You like to see how fast you can make me come? Fine.

I'm going to see how slow I can go without making you come."

He groaned in pure agony, but she slid down another centimeter onto his erection. She sat up and let her legs fall to the side again, sinking down on him completely. "Pete," she moaned as her body stretched to accommodate his.

"Babe, I need to feel you come around me." He started to thrust again and for a moment, Chloe forgot that she was in charge here because if Pete had been amazing before, he was simply breathtaking now.

Because he was filling her and she wasn't sure she'd ever felt anything so good, so *right*.

Pete Wellington had always been the wrong man. How had he become the right one?

His hands went to her breasts again, tweaking her nipples and making her moan. "Come with me, Chloe." It wasn't a request—it was an order.

She laced her fingers with his and then kissed his knuckles. "Slow, Pete," she told him when he tried to go faster. "I want this to last."

If it were possible for him to look insulted and aroused at the same time, he did. "This isn't a one-time thing, Chloe." His voice was rough with need and that, combined with the way he was moving inside of her, made her shudder. "It can't be."

She shook her head. "Tonight." She used his arms to balance herself, unable to keep her slow pace as he drove her mad. Again. "Just tomorrow morning."

Suddenly, he pulled her down, chest to chest, and

kissed her fiercely. Light exploded behind Chloe's eyes as she went stiff and then completely limp, a climax unlike anything she'd ever experienced before. She collapsed on top of him and in seconds, he had her on her back and was pounding into her, saying, "God, Chloe—yes!" Then, with a grunt that was almost a shout, he buried himself inside her and it was all she could do to hold on to him, to hold on to herself. When he fell onto her, she wrapped her arms and legs around him and held on. Breathing hard, they lay there in silence.

Had she thought the orgasm against the side of his truck was good? Or the one a few minutes ago against the wall? She'd had no idea, had she?

Now what was she supposed to do with him? There was no going back to the way they'd been before. She'd known that going in, but she hadn't counted on how much sex with Pete would change her.

He propped himself up on one elbow and stared down at her. "My God, Chloe," he said, his voice a reverent whisper as he touched her cheek with the tips of his fingers. There was no deception in his eyes, no hidden joke at her expense. Nothing but a swell of emotions that made her breath catch in her throat because being with Pete had changed everything.

Because she wasn't the same. She would *never* be the same.

Oh, no. What had she done?

Ten

While Chloe used the bathroom, Pete took care of the condom and chugged the now-warm wine so he could pour her a fresh glass. He moved the ice bucket to the nightstand, then put the chocolate next to it. There. Everything was in easy reach. Including the condoms.

It was easier to do these small things than to think about what had just happened. What, God willing, would happen again. Soon.

He'd made love to Chloe Lawrence. He was a little fuzzy on the details, but he was pretty sure they'd even managed to have an argument in the middle of sex.

Had he really told her he didn't want this night—

and tomorrow morning—to be a one-time thing? And had she really told him this was all that could be?

Idiot. He scrubbed his hand over his face, which was a mistake because he could smell her scent on his skin. He'd promised her one night. He was pushing his luck with one night and one morning. Asking—*demanding*—anything more was tantamount to failure.

Because how was he supposed to push Chloe out of the rodeo while he was having sex with her? And not just any old sex. The kind of sex that overrode every single one of his plans and intentions. The kind of sex that made him forget the last ten damned years.

Shit.

This was the problem with being scrupulously un-scrupulous. Because he knew he could very well be at Chloe's beck and call in the bedroom and still push her out of the All-Stars. It'd make everything easier because she might assume their physical closeness would mean he couldn't pull the trigger. It'd be easy.

But it wouldn't be right. If he were going to steal his rodeo back, he didn't want to muddy the issue with emotions, dammit. Sex was fine. Everyone enjoyed a good time and that was that.

Or that was *supposed* to be that.

But just then, the bathroom door opened. Chloe came back out and even though she'd put the gray nightie back on, his heart skipped a beat and he was already pulling her into his arms and burying his nose in her hair and sighing in relief when she hugged him back.

Stupid emotions. They were going to ruin everything.

Somehow, he managed to break away. He couldn't think and touch her at the same time. "Wine," he said gruffly as he handed her the glass. "Chocolate is here, ice cream is in the fridge. I'm going to take a quick shower."

She blinked up at him and he was more than relieved that she looked dazed. Thank God he wasn't the only one left reeling by the best sex he'd ever had.

He was to the bathroom door—moving quickly, *not* running away from her—when she said, "Pete?"

He just needed another few minutes to figure out how to put all these damned feelings on lockdown and then he'd be happy to work under her again. But if she asked him to hold her right now, he knew he'd be at her beck and call. Happily.

As it was, he managed to stop and look back at her without rushing to her side. "Yeah, hon?"

She had the wine almost against her lips and she shot a look at him over the glass that made his pulse began to pound again. "Don't make me wait."

He didn't even bother to fight the groan that ripped itself out of his chest. He all but tripped over his own damned tongue into the bathroom and proceeded to take the world's fastest shower.

He needed to get a grip on something other than Chloe's amazing body. Making love to her wasn't a detour, it was…just a speed bump. He could do exactly what he'd told her he could—keep whatever happened in this room separate from whatever happened at the rodeo. He didn't need to revise his plans. All he needed to do was make sure that neither of them got tangled up in emotions. Simple.

But *simple* wasn't why he barely toweled off and hurriedly rushed through brushing his teeth. *Simple* wasn't why he didn't even bother putting on a pair of shorts, instead wrapping a towel around his waist. And *simple* had nothing to do with the way he all but jogged out of the bathroom.

It was Chloe. Dammit.

She was sitting cross-legged on the bed, her perfect little toes just visible under her calves. He had an irrational need to suck on each toe, just to see if she'd giggle or threaten him with bodily harm or what. She had the pint of ice cream in one hand and a square of chocolate in the other, all while she grinned at the TV.

For just that moment, she looked young, like a girl full of wonder and mischief.

A memory came crashing out of the past, of Chloe full of a brazen kind of hope as she'd come up to him at a rodeo and said, "I know our dads have their issues, but I wanted to tell you that my brother Flash says you're the best rider here," and then she'd stuck out her hand like they could shake on that compliment and let bygones be bygones.

And he'd been young and stupid and so, *so* angry at her just waltzing into his rodeo like she owned it, which she had and he'd…

But that was bullshit, wasn't it? He hadn't been young. He'd been a twenty-three-year-old man and he'd had three whole years to adjust to the fact that the All-Stars wasn't his anymore. But he hadn't. He'd been furious that she'd had the nerve to even try to make nice. Instead of shaking her hand, he'd sneered, "You tell your daddy that next time he wants to talk to me he shouldn't send a *girl* to do his dirty work," before he'd stomped off, cussing out the entire Lawrence family at top volume.

That was when he'd seen pain etched on her young face. That was the first time he'd watched her lift her chin and refuse to be put in her place. By him.

He could not have been a bigger asshole.

She giggled again and Pete put away that old memory. "What are you watching?"

She looked at him and her whole face softened. "I found *I Love Lucy* reruns."

That look killed him. "A classic." Was there a point in apologizing for how he'd treated her a decade ago if he was still hoping to wrestle control of the All-Stars away from her?

"This is a really good wine," she said, taking another sip. "Where on earth did you get it? Pendleton isn't known for its high-dollar wine selection."

He snorted. "Ah, the guy at the front desk was happy to point me in the correct direction." Point of fact, it had not been cheap, since the cute little wine store downtown had already closed for the night. But Pete was not going to let a little thing like regular business hours stop him from getting the very best for Chloe.

And, given how pleased she was with his choice— a nice Riesling—he was glad he'd basically bribed the store's owner to reopen for him. "I'm glad you like it."

Her gaze dropped to his towel. "Want some?"

He nodded and, losing his towel, climbed into bed next to her. She passed him her glass and he took a sip. Maybe it was that the wine was chilled. Or maybe it was the taste of Chloe on the rim of the glass. Either way, the wine was better for it.

She leaned into him, her shoulder bumping his. "Did I thank you for all this?" She waved her spoon around in what he took to be a gesture encompassing the wine, the sweets and the bed.

"Yes."

"Well, I meant it."

He grinned at her, at the matter-of-factness in her tone. "Duly noted." And then, maybe because he'd had a little wine or because his brain hadn't started fully functioning again after the mind-blowing sex, he heard himself say, "I'm sorry."

She shot him a surprisingly hard look. "For what?"

Crap. "Uh, for…you know. For being an asshole for, uh, the last ten years."

Brilliant, Pete. Way to go.

He had no idea what he was expecting her to do with that lousy attempt at an apology, but it certainly wasn't the way her shoulders slumped forward and she said, "Oh, Pete, don't start that."

Dimly, he was aware that the smooth thing to do would have been to say anything *but* an apology. Tell her how amazing she looked. Compliment her skills in bed. Hell, even asking what he'd missed in the *Lucy* episode would have been better than leading off with an apology after great sex. He knew that.

But the sheer dismay radiating off her put him on the defensive, dammit. "Start what? I've been a jerk in the past and I want to apologize for it."

She shot him the kind of look that normally he only saw on her face when Flash was doing something idiotic. "Well, don't. It's enough that we've both matured to the point where we can work well together and the sex is…" She cleared her throat, her cheeks bright pink. "The sex is very good."

He didn't like where this was going. "But…"

"But that doesn't make us friends." She looked away. "Or more than friends."

He knew he was staring at her, but he was powerless to stop. "That horse is out of the barn, Chloe, and there's no point in shutting the barn door behind it. We're way past more than friends."

She groaned and it wasn't a sensual sound. It was a sound of aggravation. "You don't get it, do you?"

That was a trap of a question if he'd ever heard one and, even in his muddled state, he knew better than to reply, *get what?* Instead, he crossed his arms and waited for her to answer her own question.

"Don't make me like you, Pete. It's enough that I

respect you and you respect me. I couldn't handle it if we were anything else." She shifted, leaning back against the pillows and pulling her knees up, as if she could block him with her legs.

It took him a beat or two to make sense of those words. Respect? Hell, yeah, he respected her. He'd seen her in a new light in the last few weeks. She wasn't a ditzy, self-absorbed teenager whose only concern was how many people liked her. She was a business-focused horsewoman with big plans and the numbers to back up those plans. She put the All-Stars ahead of her family, for God's sake. He never would have believed it if he hadn't seen her handle the Flash debacle with his own eyes.

But this *whatever* between them? This wasn't respect. This was white-hot attraction that went beyond professional courtesy and far beyond their messy history.

What did she mean, she couldn't handle it?

He was going to find out, by God. He reached over her to grab the remote and shut the TV off. "Hey," she said, her voice muffled as he practically sprawled on top of her. "I was watching that!"

"Lucy gets a crazy idea, Ricky gets mad and yells in rapid Spanish, Fred and Ethel save their bacon and everyone lives happily ever after," he said, taking her wine and ice cream and half setting, half throwing them onto the nightstand.

"Pete?"

Good. Better. She was a little nervous now. She should be, after saying they couldn't be friends right after she'd ridden him better than any bucking bronco, by God.

He *knew* all the reasons they couldn't be friends. He was going to screw her over in a nonsexual sense and she was going to hate him and her brothers might try to kill him. They could *not* be friends. Not in this lifetime, not in the next.

"Pete?" she said again and he went hard at the sound of his name on her lips. "What are you doing?"

He grabbed her legs and pulled her down. "This," he said, skimming his hands up her legs, "is how I respect you."

He buried his face against the soft hair that covered her sex. She gasped, in pleasure or surprise, he didn't know. He didn't care. He licked her, the taste of her arousal flooding his mouth, pushing everything else away.

They weren't friends.

He found her already tight and swollen with need, and swept his tongue over her. "This is how I honor you," he murmured against her delicate flesh.

They weren't friends with benefits, either.

Her hands found his hair and she gripped him tightly, holding him against her, asking for more. Begging for more.

They weren't enemies. Not anymore.

He slipped a finger inside her and had to hold her legs down when her back came off the bed. God, she was so responsive, so beautiful. He loved that he could make her come in moments, when he put his mind to it. "This is how I love on you."

This was how he loved her.

He almost snorted to himself. This was not love. This was lust. This was emotions running high. This was them straddling the fine line between love and hate in a purely physical way.

Hell. He didn't know what they were.

He added a second finger and focused on timing the thrust of his hand with the movement of his tongue, finding the right rhythm to push her higher and higher. His erection bounced against the sheet beneath him, each contact making him even harder for her.

"Pete, *oh*..." she breathed, her whole body twisting underneath his touch. He pinned her thighs open and pushed her body to the breaking point.

They were *not* friends, dammit.

"I love making you come," he all but hummed as he tasted her again and again. He couldn't get enough of her. "Come for me, babe."

She broke, her shoulders coming off the bed as she damned near ripped his hair from his scalp. Her sweet body pulsed around his fingers, against his tongue as wave after wave crashed over her. Every twitch of her body pushed his own need higher until he was in danger of coming just from the act of satisfying her.

Three, he thought as the tension began to drain away from her body and she collapsed back against the bed, breathing hard and making little mewing sounds of satisfaction. He'd made her come three times tonight.

Three was a good number. *Four* was better.

He kissed her inner thigh and then sat up, pausing only long enough to grab a condom and then roll it on. "Yeah?"

She looked up at him, her eyes glazed and her mouth open. "You're going to be the death of me," she murmured as he wrapped her legs around his waist and fit his tip against her sex.

He sank into her with one thrust; she was still quivering from the last orgasm. His body jerked in response and he wanted desperately to let go. But she wasn't at four yet and by God, by the time they collapsed into sleep tonight, he was going to make damned sure that she'd forgotten every other man in the world. That every time she looked at him, thought of him, she'd remember how he'd taken care of her.

This was not a race to see how fast he could make her come but there was no way in hell he was going to go slow, like she'd done when she was in control. She wasn't in charge of this *whatever* anymore.

He set a steady rhythm, determined to keep the upper hand. But then her nails dug into his ass as she pulled him into her, demanding more from him and he lost himself in her.

Not friends. Not enemies. Just him and her and *whatever* this was.

She bit him on the shoulder and he knew he couldn't hold out much longer, not with the way she was overwhelming his senses, his everything. He shifted so he could reach between their bodies and press her right…there.

She bit him again, harder, muffling her screams of pleasure against his skin, and he gave up the fight. He surrendered to the way her body pulled him in, to the way she felt surrounding him, to the indescribable pleasure of his climax deep inside of her.

He was hers.

Dammit.

Eleven

Despite the large, comfortable bed and despite the sheer exhaustion that obliterated the need to come up with appropriate post-sex pillow talk, Pete slept badly.

Every time Chloe turned in her sleep, he woke up wanting to make sure she was still there. To make sure she wasn't leaving and, most important, that he hadn't dreamed her.

At five, he gave up trying to keep his eyes closed. He lay on his back, with Chloe curled against his side, and tried to picture how either of them were going to move forward from this. Going back to the way things had been was out of the question.

At six, enough light seeped around the curtains that he could watch her while she slept. He'd been so lost in lust last night that he hadn't properly appreciated Chloe Lawrence without her fake eyelashes or over-the-top makeup. She was simply gorgeous.

At seven, he had to get up. Moving as carefully as he could, he shifted her off his arm and went to the bathroom.

Was it possible they could pretend nothing had happened? Could he look at her ready to ride out into the arena without seeing the way she'd ridden him? If he caught some local yokel hitting on her—which happened far more than he'd thought possible—would he let Chloe deal with it without punching someone?

Could he work under her? No, that still wasn't the right question.

Could he take the All-Stars away?

He could. It wasn't a matter of possibility. The plan would still work. Easily.

But if he pushed her and the Lawrences out of the rodeo business, would he ever have another chance to count the number of times he brought her to orgasm? Another chance to save the day? Hell, would he ever get to lounge around laughing at the wackiness of classic TV sitcoms with her?

He knew the answer to those questions. *No.*

If he locked Chloe out of the All-Stars, he'd never get another shot at her. It was either Chloe or the All-Stars. There was no possible *and.*

Was that an answer he was willing to live with?

And why the hell was he trying to have this conversation with himself before he'd had his coffee? *Dumbass.*

He opened the bathroom door and immediately noticed the room was brighter. Although Chloe was curled up in bed, she'd clearly gotten up to open the blinds. "Morning, hon," he said, filling the single-serve pod coffeemaker.

"Hmm," she murmured. "Come back to bed." Then, after a brief pause, "Please."

He really needed that coffee but…yeah, Chloe was his priority. He slid back between the sheets and pulled her into his arms and something in his chest loosened as she curled into him.

"So polite." He kissed her forehead. "Morning," he said again.

"Are you coming back here tonight?" she asked around a yawn.

That was not the deal. Yeah, this room was technically his but when they went their separate ways this morning, that was the end of whatever. It had to be.

Didn't it?

"The room is yours. I can find another place to crash. One night, that's what we agreed on."

She yawned again. He began to think that Chloe Lawrence was not a morning person. "One night and one morning," she corrected.

That was what she'd said last night when he'd stupidly asked for more. He wasn't going to be stupid again.

She flung her leg over his. He could feel the warmth of her sex against his hip, closer now. "Come back to me tonight," she whispered, her hand stroking over his chest.

Aw hell. "Riders will be coming in," he said, grasping for something reasonable even as his body started to respond to her touch, her voice. "We might be seen."

That got her attention. Her leg slid off his and she stopped petting him, instead rolling over onto her back. He tried not to shiver at the loss of her heat and, when she flung her hand over her head, he contented himself to admire this particular view of her breasts. And to trace their outline with his fingers. And maybe his tongue.

"I need to tell you something," she sighed. But at least she went back to stroking him—his hair this time.

"That doesn't sound good," he murmured against her skin before shifting so he could pay attention to her other very lovely breast. He loved how easily the tips hardened to little points at the slightest touch.

She sighed dramatically. "It's not. But…there's a slight chance that one or more Lawrence men might show up at the rodeo this weekend."

That got Pete's attention. He sat back. "Is there a particular reason for that?"

He could see her trying to put on a brave face and he didn't like it. He didn't want her to have to hide. Not from him. "The meeting yesterday did not go as planned."

"The one that upset you?"

She nodded. Pete took comfort in the fact that she

hadn't turned on her vapid charm. Right now, Chloe was still very much the woman who held his feet to the fire. "It was with my family. I mean, I had a not-great meeting about the Princess clothing line, which was bad enough—distribution problems—but then Oliver called me into his office. He was waiting with Dad and Flash."

Hell. Had they found out about him and Chloe? But how? No one had so much as breathed a whisper about what had happened in Missouri last month and the whole part about them being naked in bed together hadn't happened until afterward.

She took his hand. It was both comforting and alarming, frankly, and he didn't enjoy that feeling one damned bit. "I hadn't exactly informed Oliver or my father that I had hired you to help me run the rodeo."

It didn't take a genius to figure this one out. "Flash told them." He'd had it up to here with that twerp. It was one thing for him to threaten Pete, another to beat up a fellow rider. But a man should protect his loved ones, not throw them to the wolves.

She gave him a look that was full of regret. "I might have failed to mention that Flash was attempting to use the small detail of your employment to *persuade* me to let him back onto the circuit early."

That did it. He wasn't doing another single thing without coffee. He gave her hand a squeeze and then went to get the first cup.

Which, of course, he immediately handed over to her. They were silent while he got the second cup going. While it perked, he sat down on the edge of the bed and fought the urge to bury his head in his hands. "I take it that revelation didn't go over real well."

"No," she said quietly. "Not particularly."

He gave up and let his head drop. "Just so I understand what you're saying, your jackass brother—the younger jackass—was attempting to use me to blackmail you?"

"It sounds bad when you put it like that." He spun and stared at her. Hard. "Yes," she admitted, taking a long drink of the coffee. "I didn't give in, though."

"How mad were they? Oliver and Milt?" Because Pete had been on the receiving end of their anger on more than one occasion and if the Lawrence men were well and truly pissed, they could make Chloe's life a living hell. Just like they'd done to Pete.

"Well," she said weakly, "my father managed not to give himself a heart attack, so that counts for a lot, right?"

"Jesus." In other words, he'd probably been throwing things. "And?"

She shrugged, staring at her coffee. "And...that was all."

"Chloe," he said, the warning in his voice. Because they both knew there was no way in hell that was all.

"Dad made it clear he thought I was stupid to let you use me like this. Oliver wanted to know why I'd told him I could manage the rodeo if I so obviously couldn't and Flash gloated."

"Of course he did." Man, he wished Flash had just punched him. Pete would take a black eye over the almost detached way Chloe was relating this story of family "bonding." He could just see it, her being called on the carpet while Milt raged, Oliver glowered and Flash made everything worse. Three against one was never fair.

"Then they informed me they wanted you gone before you destroyed the All-Stars for good."

He processed that statement. In his personal experience, telling Chloe she had to do anything was never a good idea. "And?"

If she was going to fire him, that seemed like the sort of thing she might have mentioned before he went down on her.

She looked at him and the raw vulnerability he saw in her eyes almost knocked him right off the bed. "And I told them they were wrong about you. Because they are." She swallowed hard, her eyes taking on a suspicious shimmer. "Aren't they?"

She wasn't going to kick him out of the All-Stars. She'd defied her family for him. For the man who'd treated her like total crap for years. For the one person who hated anything and anyone associated with the Lawrence name.

And that was before he'd slept with her. Before everything had changed.

There was no possible *and*. It was either the All-Stars *or* Chloe. He could destroy her faith in him and take back his rodeo or he could stay wrapped around her and wait for her family to destroy him. Because they would.

No *and.*

No happy endings. Not for them.

He cupped her cheek, stroking his thumb over her soft skin and a few creases from where she'd slept on the pillowcase funny. "Chloe Lawrence—were you protecting me?"

It felt so right to touch her, to pull her into his arms and marvel at how perfect she fit there. It sure as hell made it easier to ignore things like long-simmering family feuds. "Don't let it go to your head." She sniffed and the sound of her trying not to cry—because of him!—almost destroyed him. "I was protecting myself, too."

"Did they say they're coming to check on you?" Because if there was a chance that one or more Lawrence men were about to barge in at any moment, he at least wanted to have on a pair of pants before the brawl broke out.

She shook her head. "But I wouldn't put it past them. Dad's pissed because I'll never be anything more the Princess of the Rodeo to him. And Oliver's pissed at me because even though he hates the damned rodeo, he took a chance on me, and because I brought you in, I've proven that I can't do the job—which makes him look bad. Funny," she said, leaning away from his touch and taking another drink of her coffee, "that no one seems pissed at Flash."

"Except you." And him. Because he was *livid* at that hotheaded jerk.

"Oh, yeah," she agreed and he was unreasonably relieved to see that fighting spirit light up her eyes. "He doesn't see it. He picks all these fights with anyone who dares even think that he's only ranked because his daddy owns the rodeo, but the moment I treat him like just another rider, he goes crying to Dad that the rules shouldn't apply to him."

"How old is he?"

"Twenty-four."

"That explains everything." Pete smiled and then he began to chuckle when she looked at him like he'd lost his mind. "God, I was *such* a jerk to you at that age."

"Don't start," she said, but he didn't miss the way her cheeks colored.

Did she remember the way he'd refused to shake her hand? Oh, hell, who was he kidding? This was Chloe Lawrence. Of course she remembered. "The odds of Flash apologizing to you are a thousand to one—"

"If that," she snorted.

"So you're going to let me apologize to you on behalf of dipshit young rodeo riders everywhere, okay?" He didn't know why he was pushing this, only that he had to get this out. "You deserve better, Chloe. You shouldn't have to take this much crap from anyone, much less your family or—" he paused, remembering how the stock contractors had talked down to her in Missouri "—or any of the riders or contractors or anyone, dammit. Not even me." She didn't exactly roll her eyes at this, but he could tell she wasn't buying it. "We don't have to be friends for me to regret how I treated you in the past. We don't have to be *anything* for me to do better by you in the future. So I'm sorry. I never should've used you as an emotional punching bag when we were younger. You weren't the problem. I was. And I'm trying to do better. I *will* do better by you."

It felt good, saying those words. It felt better meaning them. But underneath all those warm, possibly even fuzzy, feelings was a slithering sense of guilt because it was all 100 percent true. Except for the part where he was going to do better in the future.

Because, assuming her family didn't descend upon the All-Stars in the next forty-eight hours and destroy everything, he wasn't going to do better by her.

Even so, a small voice, one that sounded a little like Chloe, whispered inside his head—why couldn't there be an *and*? Why couldn't he have *both*? Did he have to sacrifice *whatever* this was with her for the rodeo?

Or did he just have to make sure she was on his side when he made his move? Her against her family? Could he do that?

"Pete," she said, her voice soft. Because she was still nude and so was he and this bed was plenty big enough for both of them and she was staring at him like she'd never seen him before. "You really mean that?"

"Yeah, hon," he said gruffly, cupping her chin and lifting her mouth to his. He could make this work. He could keep Chloe and the rodeo. He just had to be on her side. Them against the world. Because he needed her in his bed, in his life.

He needed her.

Go, team.

He tasted the coffee on her lips and that woke him up but quick. They tangled together, legs and arms and mouths all touching and moving and it was even better by the light of day than it was in the deep shadows of the night.

Chloe was even better and, heaven help him, Pete thought he might be a better man, too. Because what if he could keep the rodeo and hold Chloe tight? What if loving on her like this wasn't a one-time thing?

What if he could love her forever?

"Come back to me tonight," Chloe moaned in his ear as he thrust into her again and again.

"Yeah," he agreed, because this—she—was what he wanted.

It could work. He'd make it work.

Failure was not an option.

Twelve

How much longer until she and Pete could slip back into the hotel, like they had the last few nights? Not that Chloe was counting the hours—or minutes. Not at all.

Okay, she was. And the answer was a long time because the show at the Pendleton Round-Up didn't even start for an hour and a half. The rodeo would take a few hours, then there was the concert with Johnny Jones, a new up-and-comer that Chloe would have to put in an appearance for and…

Seven hours, give or take. Surely she could make it seven measly hours. Then maybe she and Pete could order a pizza and more wine and kick back. Because she wanted to jump his bones again but she also just wanted to hang out with him.

She liked him, dammit. Maybe too much.

She smiled and posed and told people that their Princess of the Rodeo shirts looked great on them and tried not to watch the clock. She was in the middle of posing with a group of little girls with pink cowboy hats when an icy chill ran down Chloe's back at the same moment the hairs on the back of her neck stood straight up. Everything about her body went into fight-or-flight mode, which could only mean one thing.

The Lawrence men were here. Of course they were.

She didn't let her big smile falter as she signed autographs and told everyone that, next year, there was going to be a brand-new competition to crown the next Princess of the Rodeo which, in general, was getting her one of two responses—excitement and sadness that it wouldn't be her. Sometimes in the same sentence.

"I'll still be here," she promised another young mother who said she'd been watching Chloe since she was a kid. As she talked and posed, she kept scanning the crowd.

Where were they? Or had she gotten lucky and only one relative had showed up? Please, let it be Oliver. He was disappointed in her for bringing in Pete, yes. But Oliver was far and away the most rational of her relatives. If she could make her case that Pete was helping the bottom line and also ensuring that Chloe didn't need to bother Oliver about the rodeo at all, she might be able to make him see reason.

That was a pretty freaking huge *might*, though.

A lull in the crowd showed her how far-fetched the idea of making anyone see reason was because that was when she heard it—shouting. And not just the normal yelling that went on before a rodeo. No, it was clear this was the kind of shouting that went with a fight.

Nope. Not just Oliver, then.

She did not want to deal with this, dammit, but what choice did she have? "If you all will excuse me for a moment," she said, making sure her smile stayed so bright that her face began to hurt. Then she took off toward the commotion at a fast walk. Not a run. Running would draw attention.

A huge crash reverberated throughout the rodeo grounds, followed by more shouting. Lots of it. The kind of noise that practically guaranteed all three Lawrence men were in attendance and potentially brawling in the dirt with Pete.

People turned toward the noise and she heard them asking what was going on as she hurried past. So much for not drawing more attention.

This was going to be a mess. The kind of mess that made Flash getting arrested and pleading no contest to assault look like a cake walk. The kind of mess that couldn't be easily smoothed over with some pretty words and a well-placed distraction.

The temptation to walk away was huge. She could turn her boots around and hide until the dust had settled. Ignore the fact that her family was ruining everything she'd worked for. Because why else were they here? Why didn't they have just a little faith in her and give her a season to make it work or fail on her own? Why did they seem hell-bent on destroying the rodeo and blaming her for it?

Why couldn't they see that Pete had changed? That he cared about the rodeo and the riders and...

And her.

Because he did. She knew he did. What else could explain sharing his room and the best sex she'd ever had?

No, she couldn't walk away. This was her rodeo and her family, regrettably. But she could give them a piece of her mind because dammit, she was freaking *furious*. It was Friday night. How dare they pitch this fit right before showtime?

Another loud crash. It sounded like some of the metal fence panels used to pen up the animals were toppling. *Goddammit*. She started running, which wasn't easy in these chaps.

Her only consolation was that the fight was happening behind the grandstand, where the general public wasn't allowed. The crowd in attendance would know something had gone wrong, especially if they had to delay the start of the show to reset the pens, but Chloe needed a little time before the details of the brawl got out.

She had to push her way through a knot of riders and local staff before she found them.

What she saw made her heart sink because there they were. "You limp-dick rat bastard!" Flash yelled, struggling against two cowboys who were barely able to hold him back. His lip was split and blood poured out of his nose. It was a lot of blood.

And right next to him, practically foaming at the mouth, with his face an unnatural shade of purple, was her father. "You lying, cheating thief!" he screamed, spittle flying everywhere. Milt Lawrence was so mad that he also had two men holding him back. At least he wasn't bleeding.

"That's the best you can do, old man?" Pete taunted. One of his eyes was swollen shut and, oddly, Oliver was physically lifting Pete off the ground. Chloe had no idea if he was about to body slam Pete or what. "You can't even throw a punch, you fake cowboy!"

"Shut up!" Oliver hollered. Pete kicked him in the shins with his boot and Oliver cursed with much more creativity than Dad.

Fencing was on the ground and a couple of cowboys were trying to herd calves that had escaped and were panicking in the crowd. But as bad as all that was, that wasn't the thing that made Chloe want to howl with frustration.

No one else seemed interested in breaking things up. Instead, people were recording the fight on their phones. So much for that cushion and any hope she had of spinning this to her advantage. She had, at best, thirty seconds before the whole world knew that the feud between the Lawrences and the Wellingtons was back on in a big way.

Thirty seconds before people began to speculate if the All-Stars could survive the Lawrence family.

Her eyes burned and her throat closed up, but Chloe did not have time to mourn the All-Stars rodeo. It wasn't dead yet, despite the attempted murder happening before her eyes.

That was the moment when, with a scream of rage, Flash broke free and headed straight for Pete.

Chloe moved without thinking. She launched herself across the space and hip-checked Flash from the side. The impact jarred her hard enough her teeth clacked together but she kept her feet underneath her, which counted for a lot.

Flash didn't fall, damn him, but he lost his balance and staggered to the side where—thank God—a local stock contractor grabbed him several feet from Pete and Oliver.

"That's enough!" Chloe yelled. And for once, men listened. Her family stopped screaming. Pete stopped yelling. A hush fell over the crowd.

Every eye was on her.

"Cameras off, please," she said in what she hoped was a polite voice, but she didn't think everyone would listen and, sure enough, only a few people lowered their phones. Great. Might as well play to the cameras.

"Now," she went on in a loud but hopefully not furious voice. "Anyone care to explain?"

"He started it!" Flash yelled, gesturing with his chin to Pete.

"What are you, four?" Pete snarled back, but at least his feet were on the ground and Oliver only had a hand on him.

"Gentlemen," she tried again, although there weren't any of those currently in attendance. Pete shot her a look that walked the fine line between *sorry* and *not sorry*.

Well, he could stuff his sorry ass. This was exactly why she hadn't wanted him to apologize earlier—because it wasn't enough. It'd never be enough.

She was so tired of this.

"At least be man enough to admit you've screwed this up," Pete went on.

Which of course was when Milt Lawrence decided to reenter the fray. "This isn't your rodeo, Wellington. Hasn't been for years! What are you even doing here?"

"Shut up!" Chloe spun to face her father. "I don't want to hear another word out of you—out of any of you," she added, spinning in a slow circle. "This rodeo is due to start in an hour and fifteen minutes and the calf pen has been destroyed. The show *will* go on, by God. So you," she said, pointing at her brothers and her father and Pete—and all the various people holding them back, "Come with me. Everyone else, get this pen reassembled, the calves contained and get ready to ride."

No one moved.

"You heard her," Pete bellowed. "Move!"

Everyone jumped to attention because of course they did. Pete was a man and he could give orders. Who was she? Just the Princess of the Rodeo. Just another pretty face and an empty head and it'd be an affront to the men here and God above if she dared to ask people to do something.

She was so damned tired.

"Do you need a keeper?" she fired at Flash as she stalked past him. "Or can you at least pretend to be a grown man for fifteen damned minutes?"

"Hey, I'm not the problem here," he protested, but he shrugged out of the hold of the contractor.

"The hell you aren't." But she wasn't getting into this with him, not in public. "Follow me or else."

The Pendleton Round-Up was held every year at an outdoor arena, with rooms tucked underneath the stands. She marched toward her dressing room—which was thankfully larger than a closet. Would these dumbasses destroy it and possibly each other? Yeah, the odds were good. But she couldn't let any more of this out onto social media.

To their credit, Dad, Oliver, Flash and Pete all followed her back without punching each other. Dad grumbled about who owned the rodeo. Flash mumbled about how none of this was his fault. Pete and Oliver were thankfully silent.

When she had the door shut behind her, she turned to look at these men. Her men. Not that Pete was really hers but after the last few nights…maybe he was, just a little.

"Now," she said in as calm a voice as she could because even if they weren't punching each other, she could see that these four were like gas-soaked rags, just waiting to catch a spark and go up in flames. "What happened?"

They all started to talk at once—except for Oliver, who was leaning against her dressing room table, arms crossed and watching the whole thing.

"Boys," Dad roared. Under different circumstances, Chloe would've enjoyed the way both Flash and Pete clammed up like chastised schoolboys, except that was when Dad turned to her, finger jabbing in her direction. "I told you to fire this whelp."

There was a part of Chloe that was just as chastised. This was her father, who'd been a loving dad and had done his best to raise his kids after the death of his wife.

But she wasn't thirteen anymore. She was a grown woman, doing her best to run a successful rodeo. "Yeah, and?"

"What do you mean *and*, young lady?" he asked indignantly.

Pete smirked but Chloe ignored him. "You provided input on how this business should be run. I took that input into consideration and made a decision that was in the best interests of the business. Which was not to fire Pete." She took a step toward her father. "And?"

Dad's mouth opened and closed and his eyes all but bugged out of his head. "Do you know who he is?" he finally spluttered. "What he's done to our family? What he's doing to our livelihood right now?"

"Trying to keep Flash from destroying the All-Stars?" she replied in her most innocent voice.

"Hey, this is not—"

"Pete hasn't done anything to our family that we haven't done to his," she went on, ignoring Flash. "Did any of you consider that maybe things had changed? That we didn't have to keep doing *this*?"

Her gaze locked with Pete's and for the barest second she was encouraged by what she saw there. Support. Understanding. He was listening to her and he agreed with her and that was a good thing.

It didn't last.

"I'll tell you what's changed," Flash spit into that second of silence. "Oliver went behind Dad's back and put you in charge of the All-Stars and it's all gone to hell since then."

She spun on her baby brother. If his nose wasn't already broken, she'd break it for him. "Oh? Is that so? Well tell me this, Frasier—who attacked Tex McGraw in Missouri, huh?" She used his real name because if ever he needed to be reminded that life was not all buckles and bunnies, it was now. "Who turned the most popular rider and all his fans against him and the All-Stars, single-handedly dropping take-home revenue by almost 7 percent? Whose actions, I wonder, created such a freakin' PR *disaster* that I had no choice but to hire a manager to keep the rodeo going while I worked overtime trying to contain the damage?" Flash opened his mouth in protest, but Chloe cut him off. "And for what? Because Tex insulted a *woman*?"

"That's not what happened!"

"Like hell it's not," Pete growled. Chloe glared at him.

"You," she went on, walking up to her baby brother and jabbing him in the chest, "need to grow up. You will not be allowed back on the All-Stars until you've completed your sentence for assault and demonstrated that you can control your behavior."

"That's not fair!" he yelled. "Tex started it and he didn't get suspended!"

That did it. She snapped. "Tex quit rather than be around you!" she screamed. "At least he has that option! You want to talk fair? How is it fair that you got into a fight and I'm the one being punished for it? How is it fair that I had to hire Pete because no one listens to me when I tell them to do something, but the moment he says jump, everyone asks how high?"

"People don't—" Oliver tried to say.

No one listened. Not a one of them. Chloe knew she was past the point of no return now, knew it was a good thing Pete was holding her back because she was done. *Done*.

"Did you not see the same thing I did not five minutes ago? Where I told everyone the show must go on and not a single person moved an inch until Pete told them to? You didn't even listen to my explanation about why I need Pete's help, Oliver. Instead, I got scolded like a little kid because of Flash. Why is it my job to manage his behavior, not his?" She spun back to Flash. "So you just tell me how it's fair that Dad lets Oliver run the company but I have to go behind his back to even get a chance to prove myself and, when I do get that chance, *you screw it up*? How is any of this fair, huh?" Her voice cracked.

Oh, no. She couldn't cry. Not now. For the rest of her life, anytime Flash wanted to get under her skin, he'd just casually bring up the time she cracked under the pressure and started sobbing. She took a step back and tried to breathe. She'd rather break her hand on Flash's jaw than do anything as unforgivable as *cry*.

"Me? You treat me like a child!" Flash shot back.

"I'm not—"

But Pete cut her off. "You act like a child," he replied, sounding exactly like a disappointed big brother. "You want to be treated like a man? Act like one."

"Hear, hear," Oliver added, as if it were necessary.

"And you!" Pete turned to him. "You act all high and mighty? You play God with people's lives and you don't care what happens to them. Your wife's family stole money from half the country and your father stole my rodeo and do you care? Of course not."

"Pete, that's not fair," she tried to say.

But Oliver talked right over her. "You keep my wife out of this," he said, pushing off the table, his voice deadly.

"Or what? Do any of you realize that this all could have been avoided if you'd just treated Chloe like an adult? You," he said, staring at her father, "you act like the only thing she's good for is carrying a flag. If you paid attention, you'd realize that she's got some brilliant ideas to take the All-Stars to the next level. You," he said, spinning to Oliver, "back her up next time when it's clear these two won't listen to reason.

And you," he said, turning to Flash, "if you want to prove yourself, then stop expecting her to bail your ass out when you screw up."

Yes, because talking about her as if she weren't here was treating her like an adult. It was nice of Pete to defend her, but she could defend herself, dammit.

"You're one to talk," Flash said, getting right up into Pete's face.

"Wait—" But no one listened to her.

"I am," Pete ground out. "You think I don't know what it's like to be young and angry and lash out at every single person because of something you have no control over? Jesus Christ, *kid*," he said, hitting *kid* extra hard, "open your damned eyes and man the hell up. Stop running to your father every time something goes wrong and stop hiding behind *her* skirts."

"Guys," she tried again because this was already spiraling out of control. *"Listen."*

No one did. Not even Pete. For all his big words, he was just as bad as they were.

"All you want," Flash said in an unnaturally calm voice, "is to get *into* her skirts and then, when you're done with her, push her out of this rodeo. You're using her—if you haven't already. She's nothing more than a pawn in your plans, and it's not my fault if she's not smart enough to see you for what you really are."

She gasped, pain slicing through her chest. Oh, God—was that how Flash saw her? Too dumb to even realize that Pete's betrayal was a possibility?

She wrapped her arms around her waist, trying to hold herself together.

Dad swung around to stare at her, his face taking on that purple tinge again. Even Oliver looked concerned by this announcement.

"Chloe?" Oliver asked. "Is he using you?"

She was a grown woman. She was in charge. This was fine. She was fine.

"Did he touch you?" Dad roared, because the only thing that could apparently get her family to pay attention to her was a discussion of her sex life.

"It was his plan from the beginning," Flash crowed, shooting her a mean smile. "I tried to warn Chloe but no. She said *she* knew best."

"You watch your mouth," Pete said in a deadly whisper.

What happened next was utterly predictable. Flash took a swing at Pete's face. Pete managed to block the blow and got off a shot to Flash's ribs. Dad yelled. Oliver tried to break it up. Someone punched him and he punched back and within seconds, it was an all-out brawl.

Chloe just stood there, trying not to despair. Trying not to lose all hope that this *whatever* could work. It couldn't. She'd been a fool to think it might.

Something crashed to the ground and shattered, probably off her dressing table. Oliver yelled and Chloe...

She walked. She grabbed her purse off the hook by the door and walked right out of that room, softly closing the door behind her. The sounds of the fight didn't quiet down, which meant they hadn't even noticed her leaving. Because, when it got down to brass tacks, she wasn't relevant to the feud. She was merely another sore spot to fight over, just like the All-Stars.

Did she even matter? To any of them?

She *so* wanted the answer to be yes. She wanted to believe, with her heart and soul, that she mattered to Pete. She had the last few nights, after all.

But Flash's words echoed in her ears as she wove her way through the arena grounds, ignoring the people who called her name. It didn't matter if she responded to them or not. They wouldn't listen until her orders came out of Pete's mouth.

When had she lost track of the fact that Pete was a Wellington, first and foremost? She'd known from the beginning that he was plotting to get his rodeo back. But then Flash had acted like a dick and they'd gone into crisis mode and Pete had been so damned good at his job.

So damned good at listening to her. To her big ideas and her grand plans. To translating those plans into concrete progress on the ground. To running the All-Stars rodeo.

At making her feel like she mattered.

What if it were all a trick?

What if none of it was real?

But then again, what if it were? He wasn't in there tearing her down. He was defending her to her own family. He had her back, even if no one else did. That counted for something. It'd come so close to counting for everything.

What did it matter? Yeah, the sex was amazing. And for a few days, it'd been…almost too good to be true.

Dammit, Pete had made her like him. Even now, he was standing up for her—in spectacularly wrong fashion, but still, he was trying. And she'd begun to think…

That there could be more. That they could go forward together.

She didn't care what the hell Flash said. What happened in private between her and Pete was just that—private. She would not be shamed for her sexuality, dammit.

But it was *so* much more than that, wasn't it? She couldn't run the rodeo as long as those four kept playing tug-of-war and using her as the rope.

Her eyes burned. To hell with this. She didn't need them or their "help." If any of them thought they could run the rodeo without her, they were free to do so. She had options. She was a successful clothing designer and businesswoman. She could…

Well. She'd keep moving forward. But she was going to do it alone.

But even thinking that made her look back over her shoulder. Please let Pete come after her. If he really wanted her and not just the damned rodeo, let him come with her. Because it was one thing to say that he was going to do better by her. It was another thing for him to put action behind those words.

Please, she thought. *Come back to me tonight. Every night.* Please.

The crowds parted and she held her breath, but Pete didn't appear. Even above the din of the animals and people getting ready for the show, she thought she heard a howl of pain and a huge crash.

Right. Pete wasn't coming for her. He'd rather brawl over the All-Stars.

Fine. She didn't need this. She didn't need them. Not even Pete.

She kept walking. Right out of the arena grounds, all the way to where she'd parked. She just kept going.

Would they notice she was gone? Would they even care?

The question made her cringe and here, in the safety of her car, she felt the first tears begin to fall. Because as bad as that question was, it wasn't *the* question.

No, that was this—would Pete care?

Or would he be glad because she'd ceded the field to him? She'd admitted that she couldn't handle the All-Stars or her family. She was done.

After all this time, he'd finally gotten what he wanted.

He'd gotten rid of the Princess of the Rodeo.

Thirteen

Pete sat on the floor, his legs sprawled out in front of him as he tried to take stock.

He couldn't see out of his left eye, it was that swollen. His nose was broken for sure. Two of his teeth were loose but his jaw still moved like it was supposed to. Unlike his right hand—probably a broken bone or three there. And his ribs—damn, breathing hurt. Whoever'd caught him in the ribs had a hell of a punch. Or had he been kicked? Lord. Pete had been stepped on by bulls that hadn't hurt him this much.

A stillness settled over the dressing room, quiet except for the sounds of wet breathing. Pete coughed, tasted blood. He rolled his head to the side, trying to get his good eye to focus. Flash had come to rest against the door. His face looked like it'd been through a meat grinder. Oliver was next to the tipped clothing rack that held Chloe's dress for the evening, holding his wrist and moaning softly, a black eye blooming on his face. Milt was in the only chair still standing, leaning his head against his hands. Blood trickled out of the corner of his mouth, but he didn't look as bad as his sons. As much as Pete hated the old man, he hoped he hadn't hurt him too much.

And Chloe...

Wait. "Where's Chloe?"

"What?" Milt said, lifting his head.

"Chloe. Your daughter." Panic began to flare in his chest. Pete pushed himself up but had to sit back down when his head spun dangerously. "Where is she?"

"Gone," Flash said. He sounded funny and he wasn't moving his mouth—yeah, Pete had broken his jaw.

That he didn't feel bad about. But Chloe wasn't in here and as the adrenaline from the fight began to fade, worry replaced it. "Gone where?"

Flash shrugged and winced.

Pete rested his head on the wall, trying to think. It wasn't easy—his whole face felt like he'd run into a brick wall with it. Repeatedly.

She'd brought them back here so they could sort through their differences in private. And Flash had run his mouth and Milt had acted affronted and Pete had attacked Oliver's wife and then Oliver had attacked Pete and...

Chloe had left.

Had she tried to break up the fight? Of course she had—this was Chloe. But they hadn't listened to her.

Jesus, he hadn't listened to her. No wonder she'd walked.

"I need to get her," he said, struggling to his feet.

"You're not going anywhere until this is done, Wellington," Oliver said. "And it isn't done. Not yet."

Pete tried to give him a dirty look, but it hurt too much. "Get out of my way, Lawrence."

"Sit your ass down, Pete," Milt said, like Pete was a teenager instead of a grown man who'd...

Who'd possibly ruined everything.

Chloe was gone and there was no way in hell her family could be reasoned with, not after that fight. "I'm going after her."

Milt waved a dismissive hand. "Chloe can take care of herself and Oliver's right—we're not done yet."

"I'm done with you. With all of you." Pete tried to get to his feet again, but his boots slipped on something wet and he landed back on his ass with a dull groan. "But not with her."

Dear God, he hoped she wasn't done with him.

He hadn't meant to let things get this far. He'd wanted Chloe to be on his side when he confronted Milt, Oliver and Flash. He'd wanted to even the odds. But Flash had a way of making a man lose all sense of reason and besides, Pete hadn't thrown the first punch. He never did.

But he always threw the last one.

"I'm too old for this," Milt said, leaning back in

his chair. A nasty bruise was forming along his jaw. "This is exactly why I kicked you off the circuit."

Pete gaped at the older man. "What?"

Because he'd been a hothead back then, but he hadn't brawled like this. The room was trashed—clothing scattered, furniture tipped, the mirror over the dressing table broken. Someone was going to have a lot of bad luck. Pete hoped it wasn't him. "I didn't fight like this and you know it."

"Not that," Milt scoffed and then grimaced. "Didn't like how you and Chloe looked at each other. Even back then, I could see it."

"See *what*?" This didn't make any sense. Pete hadn't been anything but a jerk to her. "How did we look at each other?"

"There's a thin line between love and hate, young man," Milt explained, sounding reasonable—for once. "Young, good-looking buck like you? I'm not blind. She had a crush on you something fierce and it was only a matter of time before you took advantage of that." He tried to look mean. "When you tried to buy the circuit off me and said she could keep riding as the Princess—that's when I knew I couldn't risk my daughter with you." Given all the bruising, Milt still managed to put a lot of heat into his glare. "And what do you know, I was right about that, wasn't I?"

"I'm going to be sick," Flash moaned, although who could tell if that was because Pete had landed a few punches to the gut or because the idea of Pete and Chloe together was too much for him.

Oliver explained, "So Flash and I taught her how to fight, in case…"

In case Pete ever cornered her. So that was why she could throw a punch. Because of him. Anger burned through him all over again. These men saw nothing but the worst in him. "I never took advantage of her." At least, not in a sexual sense. Not then, not now.

How could he have missed that Chloe had had a crush on him? And he'd treated her like crap. He owed her a better apology. But right alongside that thought was another. "That's why you kicked me out?"

He was having trouble putting all the pieces together right now. He managed to get one hand lifted to the back of his head. It came away wet. That explained the headache.

"Well, that and you were trying to turn the local rodeo boards against me," Milt went on. "Then you sued me and I sued you back and—"

"*That* I remember," Pete said quietly.

But…Chloe?

Where was she? He needed her.

"And it was a huge mess," Oliver finished. "The feud was doing real damage to both Lawrence Energies' bottom line and the All-Stars. So I mounted a semi-hostile takeover."

"Can't say it was a bad thing," Milt agreed, sounding not even a little put out. "Retirement suits me just fine."

"Wait, wait." Pete had actually succeeded in getting the All-Stars away from Milt? Four damned years ago? And he was just now finding out? "So who owns the All-Stars? Or is it just a part of the energy company?"

"Not me," Flash mumbled.

"Flash sold his stake to Chloe when he started riding. I insisted," Oliver translated. "And I bought Dad out."

"Impudent whelp," Milt said to Oliver, sounding both angry and proud at the same time. "Outmaneuvered by my own son."

"I see," Pete said, even though he didn't.

His pounding head wasn't helping anything, but how did this make sense? If Chloe and Oliver were the only two Lawrences who owned the circuit, then Pete hadn't been trying to steal it from Milt. He'd been trying to steal it out from under Chloe.

"How the hell did we get here?" he asked, mostly to himself.

Flash groaned again, but Oliver was the one who answered. "Davey Wellington, may he rest in peace, was a lousy poker player and Dad had a massive midlife crisis."

"For a good reason," Milt said quietly, his hands clasped in what looked like prayer.

"I'm sorry for your loss," Pete said weakly. He knew that Milt had lost his wife, but he hadn't realized how much it still affected the old man.

"Appreciate that," Milt went on in that same quiet voice.

Oliver righted a second chair and dropped into it.

"What are you doing here, Wellington? Honestly. I don't want to have to beat you up again."

"You can try," Pete replied, but he hurt too much to put any menace into it. He tested out his loose teeth. They still felt attached, just wobbly. "I'm helping Chloe run the rodeo."

This pronouncement was met with a palpable distrust, even though no one said anything.

"Well, I am," Pete went on defensively. "Rodeo is a family but ever since my dad lost that poker game, you guys have run this as a vanity project."

"Screw you," Flash mumbled from the side, but he didn't say anything else. Pete considered breaking his jaw more often.

"You," Pete went on, pointing to Milt, "you made friends here, but you didn't know a damned thing about running a rodeo. You," he pointed at Oliver, "can't be bothered with anything other than the bottom line, leaving all the work to Chloe. And for some reason, that includes managing *him*," he said, pointing at Flash. "And you treat the All-Stars like it's your personal playground, where you make up the rules. None of you *care* about the rodeo, not like Chloe does."

"You mean, not like *you* do, you whelp," Milt said, but he was rubbing his temples as he said it.

Pete refused to rise to that piece of bait. "Not like *Chloe* does. When was the last time any of you noticed everything she does? Maybe thanked her for all her hard work?"

"Man, I hate you," Flash replied, but he sounded tired.

Pete could ignore the small barbs. He was a bigger man than that. Also, he was pretty sure his hand was broken. "I mean, yeah she's aware that I want the All-Stars back."

"Bastard," Milt growled. Given that they'd all beaten the hell out of each other, the older man still managed to make it sound menacing.

"You can call me all the names you want, but you're going to listen to me—the way you should have listened to your own daughter."

All three men looked at him. They weren't happy about it, but they were paying attention. Why couldn't they give Chloe this chance?

"She knew damned well my showing up wasn't an accident, but she couldn't get the stock contractors to listen to her ideas. Then Flash beat the hell out of Tex McGraw. You don't seem to realize how close he came to destroying the rodeo." Shame hit him low and he swallowed. "How close we've *all* come to destroying the rodeo. I wouldn't be surprised if she washed her hands of all of us after this."

The thought left him with a growing sense of dread. She'd walked away and the hell of it was, he didn't blame her a single bit. He'd been fighting for her, for her ideas and her right to run this rodeo as she saw fit.

Hadn't he?

God, he hoped so.

"Because of all of that, she had no choice but to

trust me because she knows how much I care about the All-Stars." He swallowed, which tasted only faintly of blood, so that was progress. "Which I do."

"And?" Oliver asked, pinning Pete with a look from his good eye.

"And she's an amazing woman," Pete admitted. "I always thought she was vain and shallow and the only thing she cared about was being the Princess of the Rodeo—but I was wrong. She cares about this rodeo and the rodeo family. She has so many amazing ideas—which you'd think you bunch of ingrates would appreciate, since it'll directly benefit your bottom line. But instead, all she gets is pushback."

The amazing thing was, they were still listening. Even Flash. Unless he'd blacked out? Pete wasn't sure.

"You saw how it was. No one takes her seriously, but when I tell them the exact same thing, they snap to it. Because I'm one of them."

Because he was a man. Was that any different?

With a growing sense of shame, he realized it wasn't. She'd brought them here to try to get them to listen and instead, the four of them had pounded the crap out of each other.

"God," he moaned, closing his eye. A vision of Chloe's face, stunned and hurting, assembled itself to torture him. "We're doing it right now. You all didn't listen to her when you ambushed her three days ago. You didn't listen to her here. But you're listening to me, aren't you?" When a Lawrence took a Wellington more seriously than they did Chloe, something was definitely wrong with the world. "She's your equal, dammit. Treat her like it."

"Like you do?" Flash sneered.

"Yes, like I do," Pete shot back, trying to get to his feet. He didn't land on his ass this time, but he wobbled. "Which she tried to tell you."

Oliver was at his side, steadying him with his good hand. "Did you seduce my sister as part of a plan to push her out of the rodeo?"

"If you think I'm going to answer that question, then Flash isn't the biggest jackass in this room," Pete shot back. "I thought you were supposed to be the smart one."

Oliver didn't exactly glare at Pete, but it was obvious he wasn't buying that. A quick glance around told him that none of them were and Pete was still outnumbered.

"I want it all," he said. This was it, all his cards on the table. "I want her—because she's got a wicked right hook and she knows how to ride and she's a part of this rodeo family. And I want the rodeo. This is where I belong. It's..." he sighed. "I rode this circuit with my dad when I was a kid and that was our time together. That was when I mattered to him and then he treated it like he treated his wife and children—disposable." It hurt to admit that. "The truth is, he bet the All-Stars that night because it didn't mean much to him. Because I didn't mean much to him."

An uneasy silence settled over the room. Then Milt spoke. "Now, son..."

Pete shook his head, cutting the old man off—and

making his head spin. "It's the truth. The All-Stars has always been there for me, even when my own father wasn't. Rodeo is family and I couldn't let it go. It's my father's legacy, the best part of him. Of me. And if you'd just open your damned eyes, you'd see it's a pretty amazing part of Chloe, too. She's the heart and soul of this rodeo. She's…"

Things had changed. *Pete* had changed and that was in no small part thanks to Chloe. She'd shown him that they didn't have to stay locked in the same roles, fighting the same battles. If they worked together, they could be something more. Something good.

"I need this rodeo *and* I need Chloe. Together, we can make it something more than my dad ever could have, something better than you ever dreamed, Milt. It's…it's home. Chloe makes it home."

He hadn't realized the truth until the words hung in the air around them. But once they were out, Pete felt them deep in his soul.

Chloe *was* home.

"We don't have to like each other," he said, struggling to keep his voice level. The longer he stood here trying to talk sense into these stubborn mules, the farther away Chloe got and the harder it'd be to apologize to her. "But can't we at least agree that Chloe is more important to all of us than this?" he asked, waving one hand over the destruction of the dressing room. He had to use the other hand to hold on to the wall so he didn't tip over.

"You really care for my girl?" Milt asked after a long moment.

"I think I love her."

The room spun at that statement. He didn't know if it was love or a concussion. He braced for impact, but no one rushed him and no one threw a punch. Instead, the three Lawrence men shared a look.

Then Oliver cleared his throat. "Does she feel the same?"

After the last few days with her, Pete wanted to say yes. But there was one problem with that. "After this? I can't be too sure she'll ever want to talk to me again. And she'll probably bar me from the All-Stars for life. But if you all give her the respect she's due, it'll have been worth it."

The weird thing was how much he meant it. This was him waving the white flag and leaving the field. If he'd lost Chloe, he'd lost, period. She might well wash her hands of him, but as long as her family started taking her seriously...

This was the end of the feud, another failed attempt at misplaced revenge. He was going to lose his legacy. He was out of options when it came to the All-Stars and the Lawrence family.

He'd lost. Funny how that wasn't what he was worried about.

Where the hell was Chloe? And how was he going to get to her if he couldn't even walk without collapsing in a heap?

The final blow to his pride was that he couldn't go after Chloe without help. Or some really good painkillers.

Another look went around the room. "Well?" Pete finally demanded. "Are we going to go after her or what?"

"I have an idea," Oliver finally said.

"I can't believe either of you are considering this," Flash added. At least, that's what Pete thought he said.

"However—if she says no…" Milt jabbed a finger in Pete's direction. "Then you're gone. This is a one-time-only deal."

Wait, what? What was she saying no to? How was whatever they were talking about different from her leaving them to figure things out on their own?

Yeah, Pete had missed something. And it might be the head trauma, but it sure as hell sounded like her family was maybe going to help him? He had a sinking feeling that he was going to need all the help he could get.

"Fine. What's the deal?"

"I don't know about anyone else," Oliver said, awkwardly pulling out his phone with one hand while he cradled the other hand against his chest, "but I need to go to the hospital. We can discuss it on the way there. But don't screw up this *whatever* there is between you two, Wellington."

Pete just managed not to smile at that *whatever*.

Probably because his lip was busted in three, maybe four places. "I won't."

He hoped.

Man, he hoped.

Fourteen

"Do you mind if I drink?" Chloe said to Renee Lawrence as she carried the tray out to the porch, where Renee had somewhat uncomfortably wedged her enormous pregnant belly into one of Chloe's rocking chairs.

It was still hard to think of her oldest, dearest friend as a Lawrence. Renee and Oliver had only been married for a few months and Renee was now only a few weeks shy of her due date.

"Help yourself," Renee said with a soft smile, waving her hand toward the tray that held Chloe's longneck beer and a pitcher of iced tea for Renee. "Drink one for me while you're at it."

"Thanks."

Because Chloe needed a drink. It'd been three

days since she'd walked away from the disaster at the rodeo and she hadn't heard a single thing from Pete. Or her family. But that was fine. She needed a break from overprotective, bullheaded male relatives.

Did she need a break from Pete?

Renee rubbed the side of her belly and winced. "I still can't believe Oliver flew all the way to Oregon to start a fight. I can barely get him to go to work. He's terrified that I'll go into labor without him."

Chloe nodded meaningfully. "Because he has so much experience delivering babies."

She and Renee looked at each other and burst out laughing because of course Oliver had never had a single thing to do with pregnancy before Renee had walked into his life. No, he was just a control freak. Which was exactly why he'd gone to Oregon. He must have thought he could control Chloe, too.

So typical.

Renee clutched her belly as she giggled. "Careful or you'll make me pee," she warned, which set Chloe off again.

She was happy for her brother and Renee. It'd always been her fondest wish growing up that Renee could be her sister and now she was. But there was something about the way Renee stroked her huge belly that made Chloe want to cry.

She'd never wanted a baby before, beyond a general *maybe someday* feeling. She'd never had a guy who'd inspired her to move past that feeling. But Pete…

But nothing.

Pete had gotten sucked back into his personal feud instead of putting the rodeo first.

Instead of putting her first.

And he hadn't even bothered to call or text since she'd walked away. Which made his feelings really clear. He liked her, sure. They were great in bed together. But she would never be the most important thing in his life and Chloe wasn't about to settle for anything less than everything.

"Do you want to talk about it?" Renee asked, snapping Chloe out of her thoughts.

"Not really."

"Hmm." Renee sipped at her tea.

That *not really* lasted all of thirty seconds. "It's just that I'm so damned mad at them. At all of them," Chloe went on, the truth bursting out of her. "I guess I'm not surprised at Dad and Oliver and Flash because this is how they've always treated me. But Pete…" Her voice caught and she had to take a long swig of beer. "I wanted things to be different. Between us. And they're not. He's the same, too."

"You didn't tell your family you'd fallen for him, did you?"

Leave it to Renee to get to the heart of the matter. "No, I didn't tell them that, but that doesn't make it not true. And because I couldn't see him for what he was, now I've screwed everything up. The rodeo, my family…everything. God, I'm such an idiot," she groaned.

Renee patted Chloe's hand. "You know, you don't actually have to take responsibility for their actions."

"What?"

Renee shrugged. "Take it from me—you can love your family and still want to lock them in prison and throw away the key." Her cheeks colored as she slid a glance at Chloe. "I happen to have some experience in this sort of situation."

"Who could forget?"

After all, Renee's father, brother and first husband had all worked together to pull off the largest pyramid investment scheme in history. Her husband had committed suicide and her father was going to die in prison. Her brother had bargained his sentence down to seven years. "Did your mother get extradited to America yet?" Because it was easier to talk about Renee's messy life than Chloe's, apparently.

"The lawyers are still negotiating," Renee said with a dismissive shrug. "But don't change the subject. What are you going to do?"

Chloe shrugged. "The Princess clothing line is still mine, thank God. I can do a lot with it."

"Big plans?" Renee said with a knowing smile.

"Always," Chloe agreed, taking another long drink. It'd be heaven—her own business, run her way, without any interfering men. Pure *heaven*.

"And what about you and Pete?"

Chloe groaned. "There's nothing to do—not with him and not with my family, anyway," she said in frustration. "Until they listen to me, what's the point? I'll always be Daddy's little girl or the irritating sister or the woman who shouldn't do anything other than smile big. Besides—" she sniffed "—it's not like they noticed when I left. It's not like Pete tried to come after me. It's not like anyone bothered to apologize."

"Hmm," Renee murmured again. "Well, I'm sorry this sucks."

"Thanks," Chloe said, swiping at the tears that threatened to trickle down her face. If she wanted to get emotional with Renee, she could. Renee understood, thank God. "Even though you don't have a single thing to apologize for."

"I should have kept Oliver home," she said, a note of steel in her voice. "Faked Braxton Hicks contractions or something. But I thought he was going to keep a short leash on Flash…"

"No one can keep that boy on a leash."

"Yeah, there's something going on with him. But," she added quickly before Chloe could launch into the seemingly endless list of ways Flash had screwed things up, "that doesn't excuse his behavior. It doesn't excuse any of their behavior."

"Right, you know?" Chloe said, unable to keep the bitterness out of her voice. "I'm not their mother *or* their keeper. I just wanted to do my job and then the thing with Pete happened and…" She dropped her head back and stared at the horizon.

The afternoon sun was hot on Sunshine Ridge, the ranch she'd bought to give her a place to get away from well-meaning relatives. Wonder, her mare, was prancing in the paddock. After Renee left, Chloe would saddle her for a long ride and maybe Chloe could leave all her heartache and frustration in the dust.

That was a hell of a *maybe*.

"And it was *so* good, Renee," she went on. "He listened to my ideas and then translated them into man speak, I guess—but he got people to buy into the changes. He didn't call me a 'pretty little thing' or say," she added, dropping her voice down in an attempt to match Pete's baritone, "'that's not how we did things when my family was in charge' or any of that."

"*That's* what made it good?" Renee scoffed. "Don't get me wrong—a man who listens is worth his weight in gold but come on, Chloe. You do realize we're talking about the same man you used to send me messages about? How many times did you write about his butt in a pair of chaps?"

"Who could count that high?" Chloe sighed, because she had only ever allowed herself to admit that she thought of Pete in a non-enemy kind of way when she was talking to Renee.

"Uh-huh," Renee snorted in a highly unladylike way.

"He was amazing," she admitted, because this *was* Renee. "Better than I'd ever allowed myself to dream he'd be. But we'd only just gotten started. Barely one freaking week," she went on. "And only because Dad had yelled at me and the hotel screwed up my room and I was a mess. Pete was there and he offered me his bed and got me wine and chocolate."

Renee's eyes were huge. "He *didn't*."

"Oh, he totally did." The memory left a bitter-sweet taste in her mouth and her eyes stung again.

"And I thought… I thought he was in my corner. I could depend on him because he'd finally let go of the past. I thought we could go forward together."

Maybe things changed, he'd told her in the bed of his truck a long time ago. *Maybe I changed.*

And maybe he hadn't. She was more the fool for having trusted him at all.

"Anyway," Chloe said, somehow getting the words out around the lump in her throat, "are you sure you should be this far outside of Dallas? Not to sound like Oliver—"

"God forbid." Renee laughed.

"But what are you doing here?"

Renee gave Chloe a sharp kind of smile, one that didn't seem natural on her face. "Besides supporting my best friend in her time of need?" As she spoke, a new sound reached Chloe's ears—the sound of tires on pavement. "Stalling."

Chloe pushed herself to her feet and leaned over the porch railing. It wasn't a truck—two trucks were barreling down her drive. She recognized her father's but…was that Pete's truck behind it?

She spun on her best friend, who was trying to get out of the chair. Chloe extended her hand and helped Renee to her feet. "Renee, what did you do?"

Renee wrapped her arms around Chloe's shoulders in an awkward, A-frame hug. "I'll apologize for this later—but only if you want," she said.

"Renee…" she warned, but Renee pulled away and walked down the top two porch steps.

The trucks pulled up in front of the house, and

Dad and Flash got out of his truck, and Pete and Oliver got out of Pete's truck and both Renee and Chloe gasped in horror at the mass of bruises and casts the four of them were sporting.

Her father's jaw was a sickly shade of purple that spread up the side of his face to ring his eye. But Dad had nothing on Flash, who looked like he'd been run through a wood chipper. He had a cast on one hand and she could barely see his eyes between the broken nose, the bruising and swelling. Oliver looked better than that, but the cast on his right arm went all the way up to his elbow and he had a hitch in his stride as he made his way to his wife.

"You're late," Renee scolded.

"But we're here now," he said, meeting Renee on the steps to give her an exceedingly gentle kiss with his hands on her belly.

Chloe had to look away. Which of course meant her gaze landed on Pete, who was hanging back. The left side of his face was so swollen and discolored that his eye was nothing but a tiny slit. He also had a cast on his hand and, as he stood there staring at her with his good eye, she noticed he held himself stiffly.

If his face was that bad, what did the rest of him look like?

She took in the group they made, matching bruises and casts and contrite looks. At least they weren't yelling and punching, unlike the last time she'd seen them. "What are you all doing here?" Chloe demanded. Because she was sure she'd remember if she'd invited them to her ranch. Which she had no plans to do, ever again.

Oliver turned and looked at the others. "Well," he said, managing to look slightly embarrassed. "We thought we'd apologize."

"All of us," Dad added, giving Flash a little shove.

"Yeah," Flash said without moving his mouth. "Sorry."

"His jaw is wired shut," Oliver explained. "It's been the most peaceful three days of my life."

Flash flipped off his brother with the hand that wasn't in the cast and she saw that his knuckles were a painful shade of purple. But Chloe had to agree—it was very peaceful not to have to listen to Flash escalate a fight.

"That's...nice," she told them. She looked at Pete, standing a few feet behind Flash and Dad. He met her gaze without hesitation. But he kept quiet.

"I should've had your back," Oliver said. "I know you're more than capable of running the rodeo and it wasn't fair to jump to conclusions."

Chloe cut a look at Renee, who pushed Oliver on the shoulder. He winced and added, "And you were doing a great job with the All-Stars." Renee pushed him again, harder this time. "I mean, you've always done a great job with it. I appreciate everything you've done to keep it going for the last four years."

"Um," Chloe said. She was completely at a loss. Apologies weren't beyond Oliver, but had he ever complimented her business skills before? Not that she could remember. "Thank you?"

Dad stepped forward because they were going in a predetermined order or something. "And I'm sorry, sweetie. I shouldn't have stood in the way of your taking on more responsibilities like I did. Your mother would've had my head on a platter for treating you differently, may she rest in peace."

"Okay?" Chloe had to blink a few times. She always got teary when Dad talked about Mom.

"You'll always be my princess," Dad went on, his eyes watery. "But you're a grown woman, too, and a sharp businesswoman and I want you to know that I'm mighty proud of you."

She couldn't reply to that because her throat wasn't working. So she managed to nod, which was enough for Dad. He gave her another shaky smile and then turned back to Flash.

Chloe braced herself as Flash stepped forward. The apology tour was making all the stops, it seemed, but she wasn't sure she was ready to hear anything from Flash.

He pulled a folded up sheet of paper out of his back pocket and handed it to her. "Read it," he got out, but then added, "please."

Chloe gave him a long look, but what the hell. They were family, after all. She unfolded the paper and read, "I have enrolled in anger management classes and I won't come to any rodeo until I have completed them and my community service sentence. I accept your decision to suspend me from the All-Stars because of my actions and won't ask to have the suspension lifted until the beginning of the next season. I'm going to work on growing up and being a better man. I am also going to quit drinking. I'm sorry I was a dick. Flash."

"Yes," she mumbled, "you were."

"Sorry," Flash gritted out again.

That only left one. Chloe looked to Pete again, but he still hung back.

Instead, it was Oliver who spoke. "Okay?"

Pete lifted an eyebrow at her, almost in challenge. Chloe tore her gaze away from him and looked at the contrite faces surrounding her. "We're family," she said. "So, yeah, okay. But that doesn't solve the problem we have with who runs the All-Stars." Or the problem with Pete. She looked back at him and the man had the nerve to wink at her! At least, she thought it was a wink. He might just be grimacing in pain. Hard to tell, what with all the swelling.

"Actually, it does. See, sis, here's the thing—I hate the rodeo," Oliver said.

"And neither Flash nor I own any part of it," Dad went on. "Not anymore."

"While I value the All-Stars in terms of market-ing," Oliver said, "I can't be bothered with the day-to-day management of it. I'm running a company, I just got married, the baby is due any second and, well, I'm busy."

"I've recently come to realize that, while I love the rodeo," Dad said, "that I was never that great at running it."

"And I'd just screw it up," Flash said. At least, Chloe thought he said that. She couldn't be sure.

"But?" she said because she was positive she heard one in there. Oliver was grinning like he was about to get to the bad news.

"But running the rodeo isn't a one-person job," Pete said, making her jump. Even now, after everything that had happened between them and with her family standing around her, the sound of his voice still sent a shiver down her back.

Dammit, she'd missed him. She didn't want to, but she did anyway.

"Exactly," Oliver replied. "It'd be best if there was a team who could manage it together."

"A couple of people who love the rodeo and treat it like family," Dad added.

"Like home," Pete said, his voice warm.

Chloe was getting dizzy trying to keep up with the thread of the conversation. "What are you saying?"

"I'm out of the rodeo business," Oliver announced, his arm around Renee's waist. He kissed her forehead and looked down at her, the love in his gaze painfully obvious. "I no longer own my stake."

"You are? You don't?" Which meant she was the only Lawrence who still owned the All-Stars? Was she even hearing this right?

But even as she said it, she looked to Pete again. Even with his face kind of swollen, there was no mistaking the grin on his face. And this time, he *definitely* winked.

"It's time to end this feud," Dad announced. "The

All-Stars will always belong to a Lawrence but now they'll always belong to a Wellington, too. It's right."

Chloe's legs wobbled and she had to grab on to the porch railing to hold herself up. "You sold your stake to Pete?"

"Actually," Pete said, finally stepping toward her, "he tried to give it to me."

Oh. Of course. Because she couldn't be trusted to run the rodeo on her own. Her family thought she needed a man to keep tabs on her, apparently. All this nice talk about how they were going to trust her instincts and treat her as an equal was just that—talk.

She spun on Oliver, ready to beat a few more knots into his head. "You *gave* your stake to Pete? Without asking *me*?" Her chest felt like someone had wrapped steel bars around it. She couldn't breathe.

Everyone took a step back—except for Pete, who moved closer. "Hon," he said quietly. "Wait."

"Wait for what?" Somehow, she managed to keep her fists at her sides. But her arms began to shake with the effort. "I notice that everyone else here has apologized, Pete—but not you."

The damned man had the nerve to look amused by this. Chloe was real proud she didn't take a swing at him—but she did plant her hands on his chest and shove as hard as she could.

That wiped the smile right off his face. "Easy, hon. I've got three cracked ribs."

"I don't care," she snapped. "You all will never change. You'll never give me a seat at the table. You make a major change in ownership to the All-Stars and can't even be bothered to run it by me? I'm done. I don't want your self-serving apologies or your condescending attitudes. I wanted you to have faith in me. I wanted you to trust me. But you don't. None of you do." Tears streaming down her face, she turned on Pete. "Not even you, Wellington. I hope you're happy. You got what you wanted. You can have the All-Stars."

Somehow, he'd gotten closer. The look in his good eye about broke her heart. "Chloe," he said and she heard regret and sadness in his voice.

She couldn't take this final humiliation. Bad enough that she'd surrendered. But did she have to do it in front of an audience?

"Just go," she whispered, squeezing her eyes tight. It didn't stem the tide of her tears, though.

She felt his warmth seconds before his arms went around her shoulders and she wanted to push him away, wanted to knee him in the groin—to make him pay for using her. For letting herself get used. But she couldn't because this was her last chance to hold him. Fool that she was, she clutched at his shirt, pulling him closer, and leaned her head against his shoulder.

"I didn't take it," he said, low in her ear.

It took a second for his words to sink in. "You didn't take what?" she sniffed.

"I didn't take Oliver's share." She stumbled back from him, but he caught her before she lost her balance. "I don't want it."

"But…you love the rodeo," she told him. "Getting the All-Stars back—that's all you've ever wanted."

She looked around, but her brothers and her father didn't seem to be in any rush to explain what the hell was going on.

Pete tucked a strand of hair behind her ear and then trailed the tips of his fingers down her wet cheek. "I found someone I want more."

She gasped but it didn't get any air moving into her lungs.

"The rodeo is yours, Chloe. Your ideas, your energy—you're the one who keeps the wheels from falling off and keeps the rest of us in line. It belongs to you."

Then the man did something she never saw coming. He got down on bended knee. Slowly and awkwardly, but still.

Oh, God.

"I belong to you," he said, holding on to her hands. "You showed me there was more to life than this stupid feud. You showed me what I'd forgotten—that rodeo was family. My family," he went on. "When I'm with you, I'm home. So let me be your home, too. Let me love on you for a little while longer. For the rest of our lives."

Pete Wellington was proposing. Just to make sure she hadn't passed out and was dreaming this whole thing, she glanced over at Renee, who gave her a look that clearly said, *Go for it.*

"Pete—are you sure?"

Yes, she was crying. No, she didn't care.

"I've never been more sure of anything in my life. I will always be in your corner, fighting for you—

even if you say no. I promise I'll listen to you and, when I forget because I'm a man and I probably will, you have my permission to punch me. *After* I heal," he added with a wink.

"That's… I…but what about Oregon?" Because Pete Wellington was proposing to her and she was terribly afraid she was about to say *yes*, but he hadn't apologized for flying off the handle last weekend and she wasn't about to let him off the hook for that. "It's been days, Pete, and I haven't heard from you and when I do, you show up with an *audience*?" The words settled around the silence and she realized that probably hadn't come out right. She glanced up at her family. "No offense."

"We're leaving," Renee announced. "Right after I pee." She hurried inside as fast as a woman in her condition could.

Chloe snuck a glance at Pete, who had blushed. She thought. Stupid bruises.

"We wanted to apologize, sweetie," Dad said as Oliver helped Pete to his feet. Dad wrapped his arm around her shoulder and gave her a gentle squeeze. "And we wanted to show you that we've all agreed to let bygones be bygones."

"Plus, we wanted to make sure there was no misunderstanding," Oliver told her. "I did offer my stake to Pete—after we all got done beating the crap out of each other. But he was right." Oliver pulled a folded manila envelope out of his back pocket and handed it over to her. "You'll need to come into the office to sign all the paperwork, but the All-Stars is yours."

"Damned impressed, really," Dad drawled, giving Pete a long look. "I reckon he might just be good enough for you, after all."

"Daddy!"

Dad kissed her on the cheek. "But the decision is yours, sweetie. Yes, no, maybe—it doesn't matter. We'll back you up because we love you. Always." He kissed her on the cheek again. "We want you to be happy. It's all your mother and I ever wanted for you and if a Wellington is the one who does it, then we'll welcome him to the family."

"With minimal fistfights," Flash said. Or at least it sounded like he said that. Oh, she was going to enjoy the weeks of near silence.

She hugged her father and then Oliver and settled for carefully patting Flash on the least-injured-looking shoulder. Then Renee came back out and hugged Chloe again and whispered, "Do what you want but remember—*chaps*."

Chloe giggled. "Call me when you go into labor," she told Renee, then Oliver was helping Renee into her car and Flash and Dad were climbing into Dad's truck and suddenly, she and Pete were alone.

Finally.

When the last sounds of the vehicles had faded, Chloe took a deep breath and turned to Pete. She was startled to realize he was holding her hand, their fingers laced together as if they'd always been that way.

"Well," she started but that was as far as she got

before he pulled her into his chest and kissed her with so much passion and need that her knees got all wobbly again.

"Babe," he murmured against her lips as his arms went around her. His hard cast dug into her back but she didn't care. "Marry me. *Please.*"

"No more fighting with my family," she replied, pulling him toward the house, her hands already at the buttons on his shirt.

"No more fighting," he agreed. "I think we got it all out of our systems."

He pulled her shirt over her head just inside the front door. "And you'll ride the circuit with me?"

"I'll manage the show, but it's your rodeo." She got his shirt over his cast and then he spun her around to get her bra undone. "What you say, goes."

"And..." She swallowed, suddenly shy as he stared at her breasts. "And you'll love me?"

He stepped into her, staring down at her with a look she recognized. It was the same look that'd been on Oliver's face when he'd looked at Renee.

It was love.

"Always," he said, gingerly touching his forehead to hers. "I plan to show you every single day for the rest of our lives how much I love you." He swallowed. "If you'll let me. Will you let me?"

She touched his face, carefully stroking his bruises and then leaning up on her tiptoes to kiss the less damaged side. "Come back to me tonight," she whispered. "Come back to me every night, Pete. For the rest of our lives."

Rodeos and hotels and ranches—and Pete by her side.

"I'm yours," he said, a solemn promise.

She knew he'd keep it.

Epilogue

Flash Lawrence smiled at the buckle bunny who'd sent him a drink. Blonde and buxom, she was everything he normally looked for in a one-night stand, especially when she batted her eyelashes and thrust out those amazing breasts. Her offer couldn't be clearer.

So why didn't he take her up on it?

Instead of asking her for a dance, which would've turned into another dance, then a trip to her place or his hotel or, hell, even his pickup truck parked outside this bar in Topeka, he tipped his hat and turned away.

"Send her a beer," he told the bartender who'd given him the woman's drink. Then he paid his tab—Sprite was cheap—and headed out.

What the hell was wrong with him? This was his

life—riding in the All-Around All-Stars, racking up the points to make a run at a world ranking and then, when the dust had settled, hitting the bars and enjoying the ladies to the fullest extent allowed by law.

At least, it had been his life last season, before he'd screwed everything up. But not this year. Not anymore.

Instead, he climbed into the cab of his truck, dropped his hat on the seat next to him and pulled out his phone.

She hadn't texted. Of course she hadn't. Why would she?

Logically, he knew why. Yes, he and Brooke Bonner had shared one of the most electric thirty-six hours of his life. It wasn't an exaggeration to say that she'd left him a changed man.

But that was a year ago. Brooke probably didn't remember their wild night together at the All-Stars rodeo in Fort Worth last year, right before Flash had spun completely out of control.

Brooke had gone on to tour five other countries after that show. Her album had hit in a major way. She'd won Grammys and CMA awards and broken sales records. Hell, she'd even made the covers of several high-fashion magazines. All Flash had done in that time was almost destroy his rodeo riding career, trash his relationships with his family and accrue way too many legal bills.

So yeah, he could see how one night with a cowboy might have slipped her mind. Or she'd looked him up online and found nothing but the headlines.

One glance at his conviction for assault and she'd probably decided to pass. He couldn't blame her for that. The best possible option was that she thought of him the way he thought of all the ladies he'd danced around—with a fond smile and nothing else.

Brooke Bonner should be that to him. A fond memory of a wild night.

Why wasn't she?

As hard as he'd tried, Flash hadn't been able to forget her, not when her voice filled the arenas in between rides, when her face smiled knowingly at him from a magazine cover every time he was in line at a store. Not when she was waiting for him in his dreams, driving him the best kind of crazy.

It should've gotten better. After an all-out publicity blitz, Brooke had basically gone dark a few months ago, reportedly to work on her follow-up album. She wasn't everywhere anymore.

Except in his dreams. Night after night, she was waiting for him, his name on her lips, her body underneath his, surrounding him. He hadn't been with another woman since her. And, pitiful as it was, he was doing his best to keep a grip on his temper and stay on the straight and narrow because he was no idiot. No woman, much less one as wildly successful as Brooke, wanted to deal with an immature, unemployed jerk.

Flash had a brand-new season to make his run at the All-Stars world rankings. He had a new grip on sobriety and his temper under control. He was going to make this second chance count.

For her.

She'd gotten under his skin, that was all. And he knew the cure—a little hair of the dog. He checked Brooke's social media—and what he saw made his heart pound.

"Just announced—I'll be at the Bluebird Café with an exclusive sneak-peek at material off my up-coming album in three days! Can't wait!"

Flash couldn't believe what he was seeing. The Bluebird Café—that was just south of Nashville.

The All-Stars were rolling into Nashville next week. If he left now…

Hands shaking, Flash fired up the engine. Maybe it was fate. Maybe it was just dumb luck. Either way, one thing was clear—it was high time he looked up Brooke Bonner.

* * * * *

From New York Times *bestselling author Maisey Yates comes the sizzling second book in her new* GOLD VALLEY *Western romance series. Shy tomboy Kaylee Capshaw never thought she'd have a chance of winning the heart of her longtime friend Bennett Dodge, even if he is the cowboy of her dreams.*

But when she learns he's suddenly single, can she finally prove to him that the woman he's been waiting for has been right here all along?

Read on for a sneak peek at UNTAMED COWBOY, *the latest in* New York Times *bestselling author Maisey Yates's* GOLD VALLEY *series!*

CHAPTER ONE

KAYLEE CAPSHAW NEEDED a new life. Which was why she was steadfastly avoiding the sound of her phone vibrating in her purse while the man across from her at the beautifully appointed dinner table continued to talk, oblivious to the internal war raging inside of her.

Do not look at your phone.

The stern internal admonishment didn't help. Everything in her was still seized up with adrenaline and anxiety over the fact that she had texts she wasn't looking at.

Not because of her job. Any and all veterinary emergencies were being covered by her new assistant at the clinic, Laura, so that she could have this date with Michael, the perfectly nice man she was now ignoring while she warred within herself to *not look down at her phone*.

No. It wasn't work texts she was itching to look at. But what if it was Bennett?

Laura knew that she wasn't supposed to interrupt Kaylee tonight, because Kaylee was on a date, but she had conveniently not told Bennett. Because she didn't want to talk to Bennett about her dating anyone.

Mostly because she didn't want to hear if Bennett was dating anyone. If the woman lasted, Kaylee would inevitably know all about her. So there was no reason—in her mind—to rush into all of that.

She wasn't going to look at her phone.

"Going over the statistical data for the last quarter was really very interesting. It's fascinating how the holidays inform consumers."

Kaylee blinked. "What?"

"Sorry. I'm probably boring you. The corporate side of retail at Christmas is probably only interesting to people who work in the industry."

"Not at all," she said. Except, she wasn't interested. But she was trying to be. "How exactly did you get involved in this job living here?"

"Well, I can do most of it online. Sometimes I travel to Portland, which is where the corporate office is." Michael worked for a world-famous brand of sports gear, and he did something with the sales. Or data.

Her immediate attraction to him had been his dachshund, Clarence, whom she had seen for a tooth abscess a couple of weeks earlier. Then on a follow-up visit he had asked if Kaylee would like to go out, and she had honestly not been able to think of one good reason she shouldn't. Except for Bennett

Dodge. Her best friend since junior high and the obsessive focus of her hormones since she'd discovered what men and women did together in the dark.

Which meant she absolutely needed to go out with Michael.

Bennett couldn't be the excuse. Not anymore.

She had fallen into a terrible rut over the last couple of years while she and Bennett had gotten their clinic up and running. Work and her social life revolved around him. Social gatherings were all linked to him and to his family.

She'd lived in Gold Valley since junior high, and the friendships she'd made here had mostly faded since then. She'd made friends when she'd gone to school for veterinary medicine, but she and Bennett had gone together, and those friends were mostly mutual friends.

If they ever came to town for a visit, it included Bennett. If she took a trip to visit them, it often included Bennett.

The man was up in absolutely everything, and the effects of it had been magnified recently as her world had narrowed thanks to their mutually demanding work schedule.

That amount of intense, focused time with him never failed to put her in a somewhat pathetic emotional space.

Hence the very necessary date.

Then her phone started vibrating because it was ringing, and she couldn't ignore that. "I'm sorry," she said. "Excuse me."

It was Bennett. Her heart slammed into her throat. She should not answer it. She really shouldn't. She thought that even while she was pressing the green accept button.

"What's up?" she asked.

"Calving drama. I have a breech one. I need some help."

Bennett sounded clipped and stressed. And he didn't stress easily. He delivered countless calves over the course of the season, but a breech birth was never good. If the rancher didn't call him in time, there was rarely anything that could be done.

And if Bennett needed some assistance, then the situation was probably pretty extreme.

"Where are you?" she asked, darting a quick look over to Michael and feeling like a terrible human for being marginally relieved by this interruption.

"Out of town at Dave Miller's place. Follow the driveway out back behind the house."

"See you soon." She hung up the phone and looked down at her half-finished dinner. "I am so sorry," she said, forcing herself to look at Michael's face. "There's a veterinary emergency. I have to go."

She stood up, collecting her purse and her jacket. "I really am sorry. I tried to cover everything. But my partner… It's a barnyard thing. He needs help."

Michael looked… Well, he looked understanding. And Kaylee almost wished that he wouldn't. That he would be mad so that she would have an excuse to storm off and never have dinner with him again. That he would be unreasonable in some fashion so that she could call the date experiment a loss and go back to making no attempts at a romantic life whatsoever.

But he didn't. "Of course," he said. "You can't let something happen to an animal just because you're on a dinner date."

"I really can't," she said. "I'm sorry."

She reached into her purse and pulled out a twenty-dollar bill. She put it on the table and offered an apologetic smile before turning and leaving. Before he didn't accept her contribution to the dinner.

She was not going to make him pay for the entire meal on top of everything.

"Have a good evening," the hostess said as Kaylee walked toward the front door of the restaurant. "Please dine with us again soon."

Kaylee muttered something and headed outside, stumbling a little bit when her kitten heel caught in a crack in the sidewalk. That was the highest heel she ever wore, since she was nearly six feet tall in flats, and towering over one's date was not the best first impression.

But she was used to cowgirl boots and not these spindly, fiddly things that hung up on every imperfection. They were impractical. How any woman walked around in stilettos was beyond her.

The breeze kicked up, reminding her that March could not be counted on for warm spring weather as the wind stung her bare legs. The cost of wearing a dress. Which also had her feeling pretty stupid right about now.

She always felt weird in dresses, owing that to

her stick figure and excessive height. She'd had to be tough from an early age. With parents who ultimately ended up ignoring her existence, she'd had to be self-sufficient.

It had suited her to be a tomboy because spending time outdoors, running around barefoot and climbing trees, far away from the fight scenes her parents continually staged in their house, was better than sitting at home.

Better to pretend she didn't like lace and frills, since her bedroom consisted of a twin mattress on the floor and a threadbare afghan.

She'd had a friend when she was little, way before they'd moved to Gold Valley, who'd had the prettiest princess room on earth. Lace bedding, a canopy. Pink walls with flower stencils. She'd been so envious of it. She'd felt nearly sick with it.

But she'd just said she hated girlie things. And never invited that friend over ever.

And hey, she'd been built for it. Broad shoulders and stuff.

Sadly, she *wasn't* built for pretty dresses.

But she needed strength more, anyway.

She was thankful she had driven her own truck, which was parked not far down the street against the curb. First-date rule for her. Drive your own vehicle. In case you had to make a hasty getaway.

And apparently she had needed to make a hasty getaway, just not because Michael was a weirdo or anything.

No, he had been distressingly nice.

She mused on that as she got into the driver's seat and started the engine. She pulled away from the curb and headed out of town. Yes, he had been perfectly nice. Really, there had been nothing wrong with him. And she was a professional at finding things wrong with the men she went on dates with. A professional at finding excuses for why a second date couldn't possibly happen.

She was ashamed to realize now that she was hoping he would consider this an excuse not to make a second date with her.

That she had taken a phone call in the middle of dinner and then had run off.

A lot of people had trouble dating. But often it was for deep reasons they had trouble identifying.

Kaylee knew exactly why she had trouble dating.

It was because she was in love with her best friend, Bennett Dodge. And he was *not* in love with her.

She gritted her teeth.

She wasn't in love with Bennett. No. She wouldn't allow that. She had lustful feelings for Bennett, and she cared deeply about him. But she wasn't in love with him. She refused to let it be that. Not anymore.

That thought carried her over the gravel drive that led to the ranch, back behind the house, just as Bennett had instructed. The doors to the barn were flung open, the lights on inside, and she recognized Bennett's truck parked right outside.

She killed the engine and got out, then moved into the barn as quickly as possible.

"What's going on?" she asked.

Dave Miller was there, his arms crossed over his chest, standing back against the wall. Bennett had his hand on the cow's back. He turned to look at her, the overhead light in the barn seeming to shine a halo around his cowboy hat. That chiseled face that she knew so well but never failed to make her stomach go tight. He stroked the cow, his large, capable hands drawing her attention, as well as the muscles in his forearm. He was wearing a tight T-shirt that showed off the play of those muscles to perfection. His large biceps and the scars on his skin from various on-the-job injuries. He had a stethoscope draped over his shoulders, and something about that combination—rough-and-ready cowboy meshed with concerned veterinarian— was her very particular catnip.

"I need to get the calf out as quickly as possible, and I need to do it at the right moment. Too quickly and we're likely to crush the baby's ribs." She had a feeling he said that part for the benefit of the nervous-looking rancher standing off to the side.

Dave Miller was relatively new to town, having moved up from California a couple of years ago with fantasies of rural living. A small ranch for him and his wife's retirement had grown to a medium-sized one over the past year or so. And while the older man had a reputation for taking great care of his animals, he wasn't experienced at this.

"Where do you want me?" she asked, moving over to where Bennett was standing.

"I'm going to need you to suction the hell out of

this thing as soon as I get her out." He appraised her. "Where were you?"

"It doesn't matter."

"You're wearing a dress."

She shrugged. "I wasn't at home."

He frowned. "Were you out?"

This was not the time for Bennett to go overly concerned big brother on her. It wasn't charming on a normal day, but it was even less charming when she'd just abandoned her date to help deliver a calf. "If I wasn't at home, I was out. Better put your hand up the cow, Bennett," she said, feeling testy.

Bennett did just that, checking to see that the cow was dilated enough for him to extract the calf. Delivering a breech animal like this was tricky business. They were going to have to pull the baby out, likely with the aid of a chain or a winch, but not *too* soon, which would injure the mother. And not too quickly, which would injure them both.

But if they went too slow, the baby cow would end up completely cut off from its oxygen supply. If that happened, it was likely to never recover.

"Ready," he said. "I need chains."

She looked around and saw the chains lying on the ground, then she picked them up and handed them over. He grunted and pulled, producing the first hint of the calf's hooves. Then he lashed the chain around them. He began to pull again, his muscles straining against the fabric of his black T-shirt, flexing as he tugged hard.

She had been a vet long enough that she was in-

ured to things like this, from a gross-out-factor per-
spective. But still, checking out a guy in the midst
of all of this was probably a little imbalanced. Of
course, that was the nature of how things were with
her and Bennett.

They'd met when she'd moved to Gold Valley at
thirteen—all long limbs, anger and adolescent awk-
wardness. And somehow, they'd fit. He'd lost his
mother when he was young, and his family was limp-
ing along. Her own home life was hard, and she'd
been desperate for escape from her parents' neglect
and drunken rages at each other.

She never had him over. She didn't want to be at
her house. She never wanted him, or any other friend,
to see the way her family lived.

To see her sad mattress on the floor and her peel-
ing nightstand.

Instead, they'd spent time at the Dodge ranch.
His family had become hers, in many ways. They
weren't perfect, but there was more love in their broken pieces than Kaylee's home had ever had.

He'd taught her to ride horses, let her play with
the barn cats and the dogs that lived on the ranch.
Together, the two of them had saved a baby squirrel
that had been thrown out of his nest, nursing him
back to health slowly in a little shoebox.

She'd blossomed because of him. Had discovered
her love of animals. And had discovered she had the
power to fix some of the broken things in the world.

The two of them had decided to become veterinarians together after they'd successfully saved the squirrel. And Bennett had never wavered.

He was a constant. A sure and steady port in the storm of life.

And when her feelings for him had started to shift and turn into more, she'd done her best to push them down because he was her whole world, and she didn't want to risk that by introducing anything as volatile as romance.

She'd seen how that went. Her parents' marriage was a reminder of just how badly all that could sour. It wasn't enough to make her swear off men, but it was enough to make her want to keep her relationship with Bennett as it was.

But that didn't stop the attraction.

If it were as simple as deciding not to want him, she would have done it a long time ago. And if it were as simple as being with another man, that would have worked back in high school when she had committed to finding herself a prom date and losing her virginity so she could get over Bennett Dodge already.

It had not worked. And the sex had been disappointing.

So here she was, fixating on his muscles while he helped an animal give birth.

Maybe there wasn't a direct line between those two things, but sometimes it felt like it. If all other men could just…not be so disappointing in comparison to Bennett Dodge, things would be much easier.

She looked away from him, making herself useful, gathering syringes and anything she would need to clear the calf of mucus that might be blocking its airway. Bennett hadn't said anything, likely for Dave's benefit, but she had a feeling he was worried about the health of the heifer. That was why he needed her to see to the calf as quickly as possible, because he was afraid he would be giving treatment to its mother.

She spread a blanket out that was balled up and stuffed in the corner—unnecessary, but it was something to do. Bennett strained and gave one final pull and brought the calf down as gently as possible onto the barn floor.

"There he is," Bennett said, breathing heavily. "There he is."

His voice was filled with that rush of adrenaline that always came when they worked jobs like this.

She and Bennett ran the practice together, but she typically held down the fort at the clinic and treated smaller domestic animals like birds, dogs, cats and the occasional ferret.

Bennett worked with large animals, cows, horses, goats and sometimes llamas. They had a mobile unit for things like this.

But when push came to shove, they helped each other out.

And when push came to pulling a calf out of its mother, they definitely helped each other.

Bennett took care of the cord and then turned his focus back to the mother.

Kaylee moved to the calf, who was glassy-eyed and not looking very good. But she knew from her limited experience with this kind of delivery that just because they came out like this didn't mean they wouldn't pull through.

She checked his airway, brushing away any remaining mucus that was in the way. She put her hand back over his midsection and tried to get a feel on his heartbeat. "Bennett," she said, "stethoscope?"

"Here," he said, taking it from around his neck and tossing it her direction. She caught it and slipped the ear tips in, then pressed the diaphragm against the calf, trying to get a sense of what was happening in there.

His heartbeat sounded strong, which gave her hope.

His breathing was still weak. She looked around at the various tools, trying to see something she might be able to use. "Dave," she said to the man standing back against the wall. "I need a straw."

"A straw?"

"Yes. I've never tried this before, but I hear it works."

She had read that sticking a straw up a calf's nose irritated the system enough that it jolted them into breathing. And she hoped that was the case.

Dave returned quickly with the item that she had requested, and Kaylee moved the straw into position. Not gently, since that would defeat the purpose.

You had to love animals to be in her line of work. And unfortunately, loving them sometimes meant hurting them.

The calf startled, then heaved, his chest rising and falling deeply before he started to breathe quickly.

Kaylee pulled the straw out and lifted her hands. "Thank God."

Bennett turned around, shifting his focus to the calf and away from the mother. "Breathing?"

"Breathing."

He nodded, wiping his forearm over his forehead. "Good." His chest pitched upward sharply. "I think Mom is going to be okay, too."

UNTAMED COWBOY
by New York Times *bestselling author*
Maisey Yates,
available July 2018 wherever
HQN Books and ebooks are sold.
www.Harlequin.com

COMING NEXT MONTH FROM

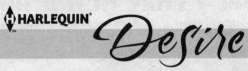

Available August 7, 2018

#2605 HEART OF A TEXAN
Billionaires and Babies • by Charlene Sands
To protect her baby daughter, runaway heiress Francesca has fled home...only to find herself hired on at a Texas billionaire's ranch! But as the secrets—and desire—build between them, she'll soon have to reveal who she really is...

#2606 LONE STAR SECRETS
Texas Cattleman's Club: The Impostor • by Cat Schield
Fashion mogul Megan was at her husband's funeral when the man she thought she'd married walked into the ceremony. As an impostor's scheme to impersonate his billionaire best friend unravels, will she have a second chance with her real husband?

#2607 A SNOWBOUND SCANDAL
Dallas Billionaires Club • by Jessica Lemmon
Wealthy Texas politician Chase Ferguson ended things with his ex to protect her. Yet now she's crashed his isolated vacation house in a snowstorm. And when a stormbound seduction has real-world repercussions, he must make a stand for what—and who—he truly believes in.

#2608 WILD WYOMING NIGHTS
The McNeill Magnates • by Joanne Rock
Emma Layton desperately needs this job, but she's falling hard for her new boss, rancher Carson McNeill. And he might never forgive her when he finds out the secrets she's keeping about his family, and her connection to them all...

#2609 CRAVING HIS BEST FRIEND'S EX
The Wild Caruthers Bachelors • by Katherine Garbera
The one woman he wants is the one he can't have: his best friend's girlfriend. But when a newly single Chrissy goes to Ethan for comfort, things burn out of control. Until a test of loyalty threatens to end their forbidden romance before it begins...

#2610 FOBIDDEN LOVERS
Plunder Cove • by Kimberley Troutte
Julia Espinoza's true love was killed years ago...or so she believes. Until a stranger comes to town who looks and feels remarkably like the man she lost. Will this be the second chance she thought was lost forever? Or another of his parents' schemes?

YOU CAN FIND MORE INFORMATION ON UPCOMING HARLEQUIN® TITLES, FREE EXCERPTS AND MORE AT WWW.HARLEQUIN.COM.

HDCNM0718

SPECIAL EXCERPT FROM

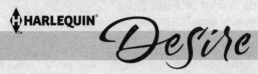

HARLEQUIN

Desire

*Wealthy Texas politician Chase Ferguson ended things with his
ex to protect her. Yet now she's crashed his isolated vacation
house in a snowstorm. And when a stormbound seduction has
real-world repercussions, he must make a stand for what—and
who—he truly believes in.*

*Read on for a sneak peek at
A Snowbound Scandal by Jessica Lemmon,
part of her **Dallas Billionaires Club** series!*

Her mouth watered, not for the food, but for him.

Not why you came here, Miriam reminded herself sternly.

Yet here she stood. Chase had figured out—before she'd
admitted it to herself—that she'd come here not only to give
him a piece of her mind but also to give herself the comfort of
knowing he'd had a home-cooked meal on Thanksgiving.

She balled her fist as a flutter of desire took flight between her
thighs. She wanted to touch him. Maybe just once.

He pushed her wineglass closer to her. An offer.

An offer she wouldn't accept.

Couldn't accept.

She wasn't unlike Little Red Riding Hood, having run to the
wrong house for shelter. Only in this case, the Big Bad Wolf
wasn't dining on Red's beloved grandmother but Miriam's
family's home cooking.

An insistent niggling warned her that she could be next—and
hadn't this particular "wolf" already consumed her heart?

"So, I'm going to go."

When she grabbed her coat and stood, a warm hand grasped
her much cooler one. Chase's fingers stroked hers before lightly

squeezing, his eyes studying her for a long moment, his fork hovering over his unfinished dinner.

Finally, he said, "I'll see you out."

"That's not necessary."

He did as he pleased and stood, his hand on her lower back as he walked with her. Outside, the wind pushed against the front door, causing the wood to creak. She and Chase exchanged glances. Had she waited too long?

"For the record, I don't want you to leave."

What she'd have given to hear those words on that airfield ten years ago.

"I'll be all right."

"You can't know that." He frowned out of either concern or anger, she couldn't tell which.

"Stay." Chase's gray-green eyes were warm and inviting, his voice a time capsule back to not-so-innocent days. The request was siren-call sweet, but she'd not risk herself for it.

"No." She yanked open the front door, shocked when the howling wind shoved her back a few inches. Snow billowed in, swirling around her feet, and her now wet, cold fingers slipped from the knob.

Chase caught her, an arm looped around her back, and shoved the door closed with the flat of one palm. She hung there, suspended by the corded forearm at her back, clutching his shirt in one fist, and nearly drowned in his lake-colored eyes.

"I can stay for a while longer," she squeaked, the decision having been made for her.

His handsome face split into a brilliant smile.

Don't miss A Snowbound Scandal *by Jessica Lemmon,*
part of her **Dallas Billionaires Club** *series!*

Available August 2018 wherever
Harlequin® Desire books and ebooks are sold.

www.Harlequin.com

Want to give in to temptation with
steamy tales of irresistible desire?

Check out **Harlequin® Presents®,
Harlequin® Desire** and
Harlequin® Kimani™ Romance books!

New books available every month!

LOVE
Harlequin
romance?

Join our Harlequin community to share your thoughts and connect with other romance readers!

Be the first to find out about promotions, news, and exclusive content!

Sign up for the Harlequin e-newsletter and download a free book from any series at

www.TryHarlequin.com

THE WORLD IS BETTER WITH

Romance

Harlequin has everything from contemporary, passionate and heartwarming to suspenseful and inspirational stories.

Whatever your mood, we have a romance just for you!

Connect with us to find your next great read, special offers and more.

Reward the book lover in you!

Earn points from all your Harlequin book purchases from wherever you shop.

Turn your points into *FREE BOOKS* of your choice
OR
EXCLUSIVE GIFTS from your favorite authors or series.

Join for FREE today at
www.HarlequinMyRewards.com.

Harlequin My Rewards is a free program (no fees) without any commitments or obligations.

MYR17